Hunting Season

The Twenty-Sided Sorceress: Book Four

Annie Bellet

D1315512

If you want to be notified when Annie Bellet's next novel is released and get free stories and occasional other goodies, please sign up for her mailing list by going to: http://tinyurl.com/anniebellet. Your email address will never be shared and you can unsubscribe at any time.

Dedicated to Vandy, for helping me wear out the library's VHS copy of The Princess Bride, *and for showing me* The Last Unicorn *for the first time.*

The Twenty-Sided Sorceress
series in reading order:

1

I carefully glued another piece of rice paper beside the
front door of Pwned Comics and Games, mirroring it
with the one on the inside. The sigil on it was something
I'd learned from an assassin named Haruki, and his
memories assured me that this bit of magic would work
like, well, a charm for keeping out vermin.

If only I could figure out how to modify it for keeping
out witches entirely. The first plague Peggy Olsen and
her coven had sent on me was to set off the sprinkler
system in my shop. Fortunately, I've got wards up to
protect my goods from water and fire damage, so mostly
it was just the pain in the ass of cleaning up a thousand
gallons of stagnant, brownish water. I'm not great at

wards, but protecting something from the elements isn't too tricky.

I couldn't prove it was witches' work that had caused the inexplicable malfunction in the sprinklers. But when you've got a coven of witches trying to run your ass out of town, every issue starts to look like a hex.

This week it was roaches. I hadn't even thought to ward against insects. I own the damn building and keep it in shape and inspected. I mean, there's a bakery next door, whose owner was possibly one of the witches. My roach problem was localized, my shop and apartment only. Thousands of the little filthy critters skittering around. The exterminator said he'd never seen anything like it outside of a big city. Around here he mostly dealt with wasps and ants.

"Back door is secure," Alek said as I walked back into Pwned Comics and Games.

"Everything lined up?" I asked. When he nodded I knelt down on the floor and pressed my hand onto the sigil I'd carefully scratched right into the boards. Gripping my twenty-sided die talisman, I pushed magic into the sigil, imagining lines shooting out and conjoining all around my shop and the apartment upstairs. I'd mixed drops of my own blood into the ink I'd used to create the magic papers, a link between Haruki's magical knowledge and my own actual sorcery.

His ability to use the sigils and this kind of spell had relied on decades of careful study and many special ingredients in the creation of both paper and ink.

I didn't need the bells and whistles to make magic work. Only my innate ability and the will to make it happen.

Power hummed in my head and a spider web of magic spun out between the various bits of paper, igniting them in purple flares. High-pitched squeals and pops resonated around the store as cockroaches of all shapes and sizes poured forth from the dark nooks and crannies of my shop only to burst into purple flame and vanish, leaving no trace but a pungent haze of smoke in the air.

"Lovely," Alek muttered.

Wrinkling my nose at the acrid burned-toast smell, I looked at the front door, still seeing the tracery of magic. Nothing remained of the paper we'd secured around the shop.

"That was cool," Harper said as she poked her head up from behind the counter. "No more bugs?"

"Universe willing, no," I said, letting go of my magic. "We can reopen for business tomorrow."

"The roaches going all vaporizy kind of proves it was the witches, right?" Harper asked.

"Who knows?" I said. "Can't do anything about it anyway. The moment I retaliate, I'm an asshole proving everything they think about me is right."

Alek slid his warm fingers under my hair and caressed my neck as he gave me a sympathetic look. We'd been arguing about this for weeks now, as the one-month "get out of town or else" deadline the coven had given me approached. I wasn't leaving, but I didn't know how to deal with the witches without being a worse bully. I could fry them all where they stood, though I only knew whom a couple of them even were. That was the point and the problem, however.

Alek wanted to go put the fear of giant Justice tiger into them. I had convinced him it wouldn't do much good.

I was the bigger person here, both magically and morally. I had to be. I didn't want to be Samir when I grew up, after all.

"Sucks," Harper said. She looked at the clock and clucked her tongue. "I should be getting home, and it looks like you two need to get a room."

I grinned and leaned into Alek's solid heat. "Levi and Junebug still staying with your mom?"

"Yeah, she keeps trying to send them home, but not very hard. You know Mom, she loves having people around. She's going to have to open the B&B again soon though." Harper shrugged, the motion too casual.

She'd almost been killed by an assassin, the same one whose knowledge I'd just used to de-bug my shop. Her mother's bed and breakfast had been damaged as well. None of us were quite sure how to handle the aftermath of the wolf council and Haruki's assassination attempts. Alek's mentor Carlos had told him that he couldn't do their Sunday talks anymore, that things with the Council of Nine, the shifters' gods, were on shaky ground right now as word spread that a Justice had tried to kill an entire building full of alphas. No one knew much but speculation was pretty wide about how that had even been allowed to happen. Faith could consider itself totally shaken, from what I could see. Even Alek's, though he hadn't said much about it since Carlos stopped talking to him.

Other than the stupid shit the witches were pulling, the last month had been almost too quiet, a calm that seemed more like a held breath than actual peace. Even Samir's stupid postcards had stopped coming.

I didn't know if it was the calm before the storm, or if this was the eye of the storm.

Only thing we were all sure of was that a storm was coming. Nobody felt comfortable. Nobody felt safe. All I could do was keep training, learn the things Haruki's memories had to teach me, keep gaining power and strength and pray it would be enough to protect my friends.

I gave Harper a hug and a promise to come out for dinner another night, then locked up the store. Wylde, Idaho dies out on a weeknight after about seven in the evening. The October air carried the first hints of winter in it as Alek and I climbed the back steps up to my apartment. We'd get snow soon.

My apartment was roach free as well; the same lingering scent of charred toast greeted me as I opened the door. The wards had been for the whole building and I was already sure if they'd worked down in the shop, they would have gone off upstairs, too, but it was still comforting to smell the evidence and see the faint trace of power hanging in a protective web around my little place. I was tired of bugs.

Alek started pulling steaks from the freezer as I grabbed a couple of candles, put them on the kitchen table, and lit them with half a thought and a touch of power.

"Show-off," he said, nuzzling my hair as he wrapped his arms around me.

"Practice," I said. "You know, you don't have to cook. We could go celebrate, grab burgers at the bar or something."

"I promised. You rid place of roaches, I cook dinner. Go shower, and dinner will be ready soon."

"You saying I smell?" I turned in his arms and poked him in the stomach.

"Like burned roach," he said.

"That's not me, that's the apartment!"

"Perhaps, but that shampoo you use will drown it out."

I poked him in the stomach again, harder. I knew he liked my shampoo and was just giving me shit. It was nice he felt like joking, at least. "If I have to shower, so do you."

"Then steaks won't be cooked," he said. He smiled at me with half-lidded ice-blue eyes, and a low, purring growl started in his chest as I slid my hand down lower and poked another part of his anatomy.

"They will later," I said, then shrieked as he picked me up and tossed me over his shoulder.

"I accept," he said as he carried me into the bathroom. The doorway was narrow enough that the two of us wouldn't fit and he had to set me down. I had his shirt off and he had mine half over my head when he froze, letting go of me.

"What?" I asked as he turned his head toward the door. Then I heard it, too. Footsteps coming up the back stairs.

I yanked my shirt back on as a knock came a moment later. "If that's Peggy the bitch librarian," I muttered, "I'm turning her into a toad."

Gathering my magic just in case, though I had a shield more in mind than a transformation spell, I threw open my door, shivering as the chill autumn air blasted over me.

Not a witch or a librarian. Just Vivian, the local veterinarian and a wolf shifter. Her thick down jacket was streaked with drying blood and her eyes were dark, tired hollows.

"Please," she said. "I don't know who else to go to. We need your help, Jade Crow."

Vivian explained very little, ushering us out the door as we grabbed coats. She told us only that she needed my magic to help her with a hurt animal and that it was better if I just saw things for myself.

"I can't heal for shit," I said.

She shook her head, halfway down my stairs already as I zipped on my hoodie and followed.

"It isn't like that, not exactly," she said over her shoulder.

"You said 'we'—who is we?" Alek asked as he followed me out as he settled his gun into a hastily buckled-on holster. He didn't bother with a coat, having told me more than once that our Idaho autumn weather was like a Siberian heat wave to him.

"Yosemite," Vivian said. "He'll meet us at the Henhouse."

"Mountain man?" I asked, but Vivian was already getting into her car, which she'd left running in the middle of the small lot behind my building. Only it wasn't her car, because she drove a truck. I recognized one of Levi's loaners and wondered. More questions for later.

I climbed into Alek's truck and we followed the frantic vet out of the parking lot, heading toward Rosie's bed and breakfast.

"Mountain man?" Alek asked me as we pulled onto the main road.

"Yeah, he's sort of a local legend," I said. "Brie is his sister or something, I think. He comes into town sometimes to get supplies, but mostly he lives out in the River of No Return Wilderness. Huge guy, bushy red beard. That's why everyone calls him Yosemite, after Yosemite Sam."

Alek's eyes flicked to me and then back to the road. He clearly had no clue what I was talking about. I opened my mouth to try to explain and then closed it. I could always show him cartoons later.

Vivian broke all the speed limits and since we were following her, we broke them too. On a night like this, it was unlikely that Sheriff Lee or one of her deputies would be out trolling for speeders. They were likely all at the diner or catching up on paperwork. The whole town was subdued by the apparently accidental deaths of the family who had owned the main supermarket, and the events that had followed among the wolf shifters.

Approaching the Henhouse, we saw all the lights were on out at the barn and saw Vivian's truck and trailer parked there. She pulled up her loaner car beside it and waved us over.

Harper, Max, Levi, and Ezee were all there, crowded around the biggest stall.

"Move," Vivian said, her voice half growl.

Everyone moved. Their faces when they turned toward me were grim and horror-struck. The air fairly crackled with shifter anger. I noticed as I passed that the other stalls were empty, and I wondered where the horses had gone.

Vivian pulled open the stall door, and I looked over the short woman's head as I came up behind her. The barn usually smelled of horse and hay and sawdust, but tonight all I could smell was blood and something rotten, like a compost heap in high summer.

Yosemite, who had a few inches and at least eighty pounds on Alek, knelt inside the stall, a white horse prone beside him with bloody gashes oozing blackish fluid all along its pale sides and flanks. He leaned back as he turned his head to me, revealing the head of the horse, which he cradled in his lap. A long, pearlescent horn stretched out over a foot from the forehead of the animal.

"Unicorn," I said, frozen in the door of the stall.

"He's dying," Yosemite said. "Fix him."

I crept into the stall. The unicorn's eye rolled toward me, his gaze dark and pained. There was intelligence there, more than I'd ever seen in all my years of working with horses. I'd been a working student at a barn once, during my twenty years of living on the run, and helped Max with their horses from time to time out of nostalgia. I'd ridden show jumpers worth six figures and trail ponies saved from auction. All beautiful. None as beautiful as I imagined the unicorn would have been.

His abdomen was torn open, guts glistening where they weren't caked with blood and woodchips. His breathing was labored, rasping. I didn't know how he was still alive. Unicorn magic, I guess. I understood my friend's anger now, why everyone in the barn looked ready to go to war and tear something apart. Whatever had done this to such a magnificent creature was evil, pure fucking evil.

"I don't know how to heal," I said. I tried to fix Alek once, to drive poison from his body, and almost gotten us both killed instead.

"He could heal, but there's something wrong. I feel magic at work, but it is nothing I've ever seen, something foul and tainted." Yosemite's eyes were multicolored, one green, one blue, like a white cat Sophie had once rescued when I was still in high school.

I knelt down, pushing my sleeves back and summoning my magic. I laid my hand gently on the unicorn's shoulder. His coat was soft and thick; it felt like I was touching rabbit fur instead of horsehair. Closing my eyes, partially for focus and partially because I couldn't stand to see any more exposed guts, I pushed my magic into the unicorn and tried to *see* the taint.

Yosemite was right. Clinging dark magic twisted and writhed within the unicorn, covering the bright pure light of his own innate power. The taint reminded me of those pictures they show you after oil spills, where the animals are coated in inky black sludge, barely visible as a creature beneath the filth.

The magic was alien to me, however. I didn't know how to fight it, or how to kill it. I pictured my own power as dish soap and attempted to scrub away the filth. The filth reacted by spreading and writhing, not retreating. Nausea ate a hole in my stomach as I swallowed bile and struggled to retain focus, to keep the magical bond with the unicorn. He was trying to fight, but his light was so dim, his own power nearly extinguished by the filth.

Fireball? No problem. Shields? Lightning? Destruction? Finding lost socks? I was good at these things. When it came to this kind of thing, I was lost. Helpless. I hated it.

A long gasp rattled from the unicorn's throat and he stilled beneath my hand.

"No you fucking don't," I muttered. I was not letting the unicorn go gentle into that evil damn night.

Turning my magic into a lance, I speared through the filth, reaching for the dimming sparkle of his power. "Rage, rage," I whispered, barely aware of the sound of my own voice.

The iridescent power touched mine and joy filled me, pure and wild. The joy of a flower blooming through the last frost of winter, sunlight breaking warm and golden through a clouded sky. The burble of a brook, clear water cold and sweet on the tongue. The joy of storm winds whipping down a valley and the quiet of a forest buried in fresh snow.

I clung to that joy, though it hurt, like staring into the sun. I fed it strength, trying to remember every time in my life I'd ever felt like this, giving over everything good and happy that I had for this creature until one memory stood clear.

It's dark and everyone was saying there would be below-freezing temperatures tonight. I had nowhere to go, so when the little Asian guy offered me a warm meal and somewhere to sleep tonight, I figured even if he wanted a fuck or something, I could talk him down to a handjob. He's pretty short and thin. I'm in a weird old house and he's arguing with two women in the other room. I try not to listen. I guess they don't like the idea of this guy bringing home a street kid, but now I'm not so certain why he did. Seems weird to pick up a kid when you already have two women, right? Maybe they are only into each other.

I'm debating what the wooden clock on the wall might be worth if I can get out of here and pawn it when the women come in to the kitchen. One starts making me another sandwich. The other sits down across from me at the little table.

"Ji-hoon says you have nowhere to go?" she asks.

"No," I say. I wonder if they will call the cops. I wonder if I care anymore.

"Why?" she asks.

Screw this, *I think, but I decide to answer her. "My family kicked me out, because I'm not like them." I give her my best hard stare. She can have the truth, but no one will ever get my tears. Not ever, not over this.*

She glances at the other woman and they seem to telepathically decide something as she nods. "I'm Kayla," she says. "That's Sophie. We're not like anyone else, either."

Then she smiles, and weirdly I know that life has changed, and for the first time in a year, the sun comes out in my heart.

The unicorn's power fed on mine, drinking in my memory, my moments of true relief and joy. Magic— mine, his, I wasn't sure—cascaded through both of us like a tidal wave of glitter. I was barely in control, hanging onto my magic through will alone, unaware of anything outside myself and the unicorn.

The filth burned away as though we'd thrown a match onto gasoline. I felt bones knitting together, wounds closing. Then the wave ebbed and the unicorn let me go. Reality came back to me in stages. First it was touch, my hand still clutching soft fur. Laughter, voices exclaiming, a sense of deep relief replacing the anger and tension. Cautiously I opened my eyes.

The unicorn breathed again, his dark eye closed, but his nostrils flaring gently with each easy breath. Blood still stained his coat, red now instead of inky black, but the gashes were closed and only deep pink scars remained where the gaping wounds had been.

"You saved him," Yosemite said as he ran a sweaty hand through his dark red curls. "Thank you." His tone made it pretty clear he hadn't thought I could. I remembered that Brie was his sister or something and wondered what she'd said about me.

"I think he mostly saved himself," I said, stroking the unicorn's fur gently. I didn't want to stop touching him, to release myself from the joy, but I made myself let go. My chest hurt and my legs barely wanted to hold me up as I got slowly to my feet. "What did this to him?"

Yosemite gently laid the unicorn's head on the stall bedding and unfolded himself. He was definitely taller than Alek. "We should talk inside," he said, motioning with his head toward the house.

Rosie and Junebug had joined the crowd outside the stall, but everyone took the cue and made their way to the house, except for Max, who said he wanted to stay and keep an eye on the unicorn after he brought the horses back in. It was a sign how subdued everyone was that both Levi and Harper missed an obvious joke about virgins as we left the barn.

"They went crazy when Yosemite showed up with the unicorn like that," Harper explained about the horses as we walked up to the Henhouse.

"Unicorns are guardians of the wild things," Yosemite said in a deep, smooth voice behind me. "The whole forest will be going mad over what has happened. It was good we were able to save one."

I waited until coats and boots were off and we were settled in the living room before I asked him what he meant by "save one."

Vivian passed me her phone as she and the mountain man exchanged dark looks filled with grief. On it were pictures, flashes of horror taken with a cellphone camera in the dark. Unicorns, at least three, ripped to pieces, their bodies black with filth and gore.

"The Bitterroot pack is guarding their bodies," Yosemite said. "I will have to try to lay them to rest, though I do not know if the forest will allow it."

"Aurelio? I mean, Softpaw?" I said, surprised. "I figured he and his would be long gone from here."

"They were, but dark things have been stirring in the wilds, beasts slain for cruel sport instead of food, spore from creatures that we've never seen before. He found me and we were tracking a pack of whatever did this when the forest went mad and I followed the treesong to the unicorns. The stallion was the only one still alive. I tried to use my knowledge to help, but this was far beyond my power." Yosemite's hands clenched into fists in his lap.

I looked closely at him, really looked, now that he wasn't bundled into a thick jacket and I had a moment. His skin was tanned and freckled, his arms covered in red-gold hair, but his tattoos were visible and looked very old, faded and blue. I made out shapes of animals, a fish, something like a cat, a stylized wolf's head, and spirals mixed in. It reminded me of the tattoos on a Celtic woman they'd found in a bog, her body preserved for a couple thousand years. I reached out magically, touching him with the lightest brush of my power, and felt the answering thrum of his own, smelling to my metaphysical senses like pine needles and the air before a snowstorm.

He looked into my eyes with a suddenly ancient gaze and I let my magic go, lifting a shoulder in a half-shrug of apology. "You are a druid," I said. Hey, if there were unicorns, why not druids? I'd always thought that Brie might be one. "Brie is your sister?"

He laughed, a quick bark that died as soon as it was out. "No, she's not my sister. But I am a druid. Taking care of the Frank is my charge." He looked away, staring into a middle distance, seeing none of us. "And I am failing."

I looked at the phone in my hands, glad the screen had gone dark, and could find nothing to say.

"Hey," Ezee said. He'd taken a seat on the couch next to the druid and now scooted over the scant distance between them, putting a hand on Yosemite's arm. "The unicorn will live, right? And now you have not only the Bitterroot pack to help, but all of us."

"It's true," Harper said. "We've vanquished a little evil in our time, for sure."

Rosie made a noise in the back of her throat, threw up her hands in dramatic fashion, and mumbled something about making tea as she left the room. If I had to guess, I'd say that the idea of all of us, her real and adopted family, running out into the woods to fight evil didn't sit well with her. But she wouldn't stop us, either. After seeing Vivian's pictures, after feeling that filth clotting and killing the unicorn's wild purity, I was ready to go lay down some serious pain on whatever had done it.

A whining voice in the back of my mind told me it might be my fault. This couldn't be coincidence. I didn't believe in it, couldn't afford to after everything. Somehow this would be tied to Samir. I felt it in my exhausted bones. I still mentally shut that voice into the closet, however. Nothing I could do but fight whatever came and try to protect the people I loved.

I leaned into Alek's warmth as he wrapped an arm around my shoulders.

"Do you want help burying them?" he asked Yosemite. "I can dig."

"There will be no digging," Yosemite said. "I will ask the earth to take her children inside of her. If they are too tainted, we will have to burn them instead."

Ezee squeezed Yosemite's arm and the druid slid his hand over Ezee's own. I realized that they must know each other, though neither Ezee nor Levi had ever said anything to me about the mountain man. He'd never really come up, since his visits to town were pretty rare from what I knew. There was a familiarity between them, the kind people only get after years of knowing someone. Or the kind you get between lovers. I raised an eyebrow at Ezee and he raised one back, his expression clearly telling me we could talk later.

Rosie brought out tea and we mostly drank it in silence. The mood was grim despite the miracle I'd pulled off with the unicorn and I had trouble keeping my eyes open after few minutes as the aftermath of using power like that hit me. I knew I'd be fine come morning with a little sleep and food in me; my recovery times were getting shorter and shorter as I got stronger. Didn't help the exhaustion now.

Alek and I said our goodbyes with a promise to come check on the unicorn tomorrow. Yosemite promised to keep us advised of the situation in the wilderness and call upon me again for help if he needed. We drove home in near silence and I found myself drifting off in the warmth of the truck cab. Alek touched my knee gently as he parked.

"There's someone sitting at the top of your steps," he said softly.

I could barely make out the shape of a person as I squinted through the windshield at the figure under the porch light. The figure was seated, but stood as Alek shut the truck down. It was a woman, in a thin coat that looked like leather, with a thick ponytail of hair spilling off the back of her head. Her face was in shadow as the porch light backlit her, but she didn't seem familiar.

"Want to go get a motel room?" I asked Alek, only half joking. I didn't want to deal with anything else today.

"Want me to eat her?" he said, smiling.

"She's probably a witch," I muttered, wondering what stupid thing they were going to try now.

"If she's a witch, you can turn her into a toad." He squeezed my knee and climbed out of the truck, letting all the nice warm air out.

Sighing, I climbed out and summoned my magic, wondering if I could turn someone into a toad. The wards around my building weren't going crazy, so she wasn't actively working magic or anything, but they hummed slightly as I checked them.

I stayed at the bottom of the steps and let her come down to me, though the light here was worse. "Who are you?" I asked.

Her eyes were dark and big in her thin, heart-shaped face. She was strikingly beautiful despite her tired look, her face made up as though she'd walked off a magazine photoshoot and found herself on my stairs by accident.

She wore a thin leather jacket that hung in a flattering way down to mid-thigh, jeans, and four-inch red heels, which would have identified her as an out-of-towner if nothing else had. Around her neck was a silver chain with a delicate heart-shaped lock hanging from it that seemed to catch the light and glint on its own.

I stopped breathing as I looked at the lock and power poured out around me in visible, purple sparks as I dragged my gaze up to her face.

"Where is he?" I asked.

I'd had a lock and chain like that once. I'd melted it off of myself over twenty-five years ago. Looking at hers, I could feel the blinding pain, the heat on my skin as I forced the magic lock to melt and come loose. As I broke the bond between Samir and myself for good.

"My name is Tess," the woman said. "Please, you have to protect me."

Wolf, my spirit guardian, appeared beside me, her dark hackles raised but otherwise calm as she stared at the woman. I let the moment stretch out and then sighed as Wolf looked toward me and cocked her head in a silent question.

I let the woman into my apartment. It was late, cold, and I was tired. I wanted to be inside my wards, on familiar ground where at least I wouldn't have to worry about a sniper or some bullshit like that. Wouldn't be the first time Samir had done something underhanded like that.

I pointed at a kitchen chair and said "Sit."

She sat, her arms wrapping around her body as though inside were colder than out. Looking at her terrified, unhappy face, I almost felt pity for her, but I shoved it aside.

"Why are you still wearing his necklace if you want to get away from him?" I asked.

"I don't know how to take it off," she said, fingering the charm with a shaking hand.

Alek growled. We had taken up triangular positions, Wolf's large form to my right and Alek to my left, both where I could see them without having to take my eyes off the woman.

"That's strike one," I said. "Lie to me again and I'll let him serve me your heart for dinner."

"All right," she whispered. "He'll know when I take it off."

That was true. I didn't even need Alek's nod to confirm it. The charm tied her to Samir; it was a promise inside a delicate spell. He and I had worn matching ones, our love made into filigree metal and sealed with power and blood. I felt a twinge that I worried might be jealousy, and angrily shoved the feeling away.

"Where is Samir?" I asked.

"I don't know," she said.

Alek gave a slight nod. Truth.

"Does he know you are here?"

"I am sure he has guessed," she said. "He likes to keep an eye on you."

"How?" I asked. It was something I'd been wondering for months now. He seemed to know so much about me that it made me wonder if I'd hidden as well as I'd hoped all these years, or if he'd been busy elsewhere and decided to finally to turn his attention to me.

"I don't know that, either," she said. She glanced at Alek as he narrowed his eyes and nodded. "He doesn't like to tell me things. Knowledge is power, and he prefers all the power be his."

I took a deep breath and forced my hand to unclench from my talisman. I had a d20 imprint on my palm that faded as I stared at it. I knew what she meant all too well. Every instinct in my body was screaming at me to fry her where she stood, that this was another trick. It probably was, but I could have been looking at myself twenty-five years ago. If I had known of a former lover of his, of someone who got away, would I have gone to me for help? I thought perhaps I would have.

"Why come to me?" I asked, pacing the short distance across my kitchen. I let my fingers trail through Wolf's fur, her strength reassuring.

Tess gave me an odd look. She couldn't see the giant black wolflike creature I was petting, so my gesture must have appeared odd. Most of the time I avoid interacting with Wolf in front of people for that reason, but tonight I really didn't give a fuck.

"You got away from him," she said. "He's going to kill me, eat my heart and take my power. It's what he does."

"Yet you swore devotion to him," I said, indicating the heart-shaped lock.

"As did you, once," she said, her full lips pressing together and her chin coming up in a new show of will. In the better lighting inside my apartment, her irises appeared to have deep reddish-brown whorls in them, her eyes taking on the color of firelit brandy. She looked like a perfect damsel in distress, damp ringlets escaping her ponytail, her body not so thin that she didn't have an obviously heaving bosom to complete the picture. She could have given Queen Amidala a lesson in distressed bosom heaving.

I gathered my scattering thoughts.

"Are you here to kill me?" I asked.

"I want free of Samir," she said without hesitation. "I think you have the best chance of anyone of protecting me and killing him."

Alek pressed his lips together and nodded with a grimace. I didn't need him to tell me she spoke the truth, though the confirmation was nice. I could hear her desire in her voice, read it on her terrified but determined face.

I sank my fingers back into Wolf's fur and closed my eyes. I was so damned tired of everything. The wild joy the unicorn's magic had spawned inside me had shined a light into my exhausted heart. I didn't want to run anymore, but the waiting was killing me, bit by bit.

Waiting for Samir to make a move. Waiting for someone else to try to hurt me or the people I loved. Waiting for the right moment, for some day in whatever future I had where I'd somehow trained enough, gotten strong enough, become someone who could stand up to him and say "no more."

I felt like the characters in the second act of my favorite musical, *Into the Woods*. I wanted to belt out the lyrics to "No More" and crawl under the covers. There was no convenient orchestra for me here, however, and I was pretty sure my audience would ruin the drama of it. No more hiding for me. No more running. No more waiting.

Perhaps Tess was a gift, a tool placed in my hands by fate.

"Fine," I said, opening my eyes to find Tess and Alek watching me, both of their expressions grim and guarded. "You know where Samir lives? Let's go. Tomorrow, you and me. If he's not there, we'll wait for him."

"But…" She stuttered, stopped, then started again, "I don't know where he lives. I mean, I know he has a mansion in a valley, but I couldn't tell you where it is."

"Why not?" I asked. Samir and I had lived in a beautiful house in Detroit after he seduced me away from

New York. He'd let me come and go as I pleased, though my freedom had been an illusion, and I hadn't wanted to leave him anyway. Not until the end.

"He always flies me there in a private plane, then a helicopter. Everything is warded and I'm always blindfolded. If I want to leave, I have to go the same way. I don't know if it is even in the States. The landscape is carefully groomed, too many differing plants for it all to be native." She spread her hands. "You hurt him, and now he doesn't trust anyone or anything."

"*I* hurt *him*?" I choked down a bubble of irrational laughter, swallowing it like an unpleasant burp. "He nearly killed me. He…" I stopped, my eyes burning as I blinked back tears. This woman was a stranger; she didn't need to know about my losses. She was dangerous, sincere or not. Having her here was a mistake, for both of us. Especially if she couldn't help me.

"So you can't tell me where he is or where he will be?" I reiterated.

"No," she said. "Though I imagine he'll come for you eventually. He's reluctant to face you. That's why I'm here. You are the only person he seems wary of."

That was mildly comforting. Very mild. Like tepid bathwater mild.

"Take off your charm," I said, forcing away any pity I felt for her. I'd melted mine off, not knowing the trick of opening it. I was curious how she would do it, and I didn't care if Samir knew she had. Let her prove herself if she wanted my help. I wanted to feel her magic, to see it.

She lifted her hand to the necklace and her sleeve slipped back, revealing a silver charm bracelet. Only one charm dangled from it, a cross with a tiny crucified body on it. Her power, when she called it, was cool and crisp to my senses, tasting somewhat like sucking on an ice-cube. She closed her eyes and hummed a soft, clear note. The air around us grew thick and still, as though time itself hung for a moment on that note. With a quick tug, the necklace broke free, sliding through her neck as though the chain or her throat were merely illusion.

It was amazing, and terrifying. Not because she used a lot of magic, because she hadn't. I felt only the merest breath of power, barely more than I had exercised earlier that night when lighting the candles now burned to nubs on my kitchen table. It was her control, her finesse, what she managed to do with so little magic.

I knew in that moment that whoever Tess was, I would be stupid to underestimate her. And more stupid to keep her around. Either she had been sent by Samir to kill or weaken me, or he'd severely misjudged his new apprentice and lover. Maybe both.

And yet I was tempted. She seemed so afraid, so certain he would kill her. Which he would, sooner or later. It was what Samir did, after all. She had knowledge of magic—I felt it, saw it in her economy.

"How old are you?" I asked, unable to keep the awe out of my voice completely.

She looked up at me, surprise flickering in her brandy-colored eyes. She started to turn her head slightly and look at Alek, but seemed to think better of it. "Older than you," she said. "I was born a decade or so before the American Civil War."

"You avoided Samir for more than a century, no?" Alek asked her.

"Yes, but I could not do so forever. He has eyes and ears everywhere. The moment anyone gains enough power to be noticed, to be identified as a sorcerer, he pounces. The pretty ones, the young ones, he keeps as lovers, until he grows bored. And it seems he grows bored more quickly with each passing decade." Her body was tensed, poised for flight.

I got the feeling she hadn't planned on telling me these things, had hoped I would take her at face value. I hadn't been around a hundred and fifty years, but I wasn't exactly born yesterday, either. She was good at deception, and I wondered what I would have done if I hadn't had Alek here to keep her on the truthful path.

"Look," I said. "I can't trust you. You fear me, too. This is a disaster in the making and we both need to just admit it. I believe that you are genuine in your fear of Samir. You don't strike me as a stupid woman and I'm guessing you figured you could pretend you were a naïve young thing for a while until you found a way to bring him down or get away. How am I doing?"

"Better than I expected," she said, the ghost of a smile touching her ruby-red lips.

"I can't help you. I am not sure I would if I could, honestly. I mean, I'll do my damndest to bring down that bastard if he ever deigns to show himself, but having you here is just one more fucking worry I don't need on my plate." I paused as I realized her showing up here and the unicorn getting mauled were probably related. Coincidences? Don't exist on my planet.

"You can help—" she started to say.

I cut her off with a raised hand. "You know anything about evil creatures in the woods killing unicorns?"

"What? Unicorns?" Her confusion seemed genuine and Alek raised an eyebrow at me. "Unicorns aren't real."

"I just patched one up tonight," I said. I still didn't believe in coincidences, but it was clear if the unicorn murders were related to Tess, it wasn't in a way she was actively in on.

"Unicorns are real?" she said.

"Yep," I said. I took a deep breath, marshalling my thoughts. She couldn't tell me where Samir was. She was dangerous in many ways, most of which I probably hadn't even thought through yet, because damnit, I was tired as hell and hadn't had time.

"You can't stay, Tess," I said, trying to be kind. "You need to destroy that charm and then run, far and fast. Don't use your magic. Hopefully Samir will think you came to me and that I'm hiding you. His attention at the least will be divided, right? So you've got a chance. Take it. You need money?" I doubted from her designer clothes that she did, but who knew how controlling Samir had gotten.

"No," she said. "I have money. But I have nowhere to go."

"Neither did I, twenty-five years ago," I said. "I made do. You're a survivor, I bet. You'll be fine. Run, and don't look back."

"I can help you," she said. "You are powerful, right? But I know magic. I've been using it a long time. We can be stronger together than apart. Two against one. Don't send me away, Jade Crow. Please."

I think she would have sunk to her knees if she'd thought it would help, but instead she rose, staring me down eye to eye. She was white, her skin milky pale, and her hair was a deep reddish-brown with a gentle curl to it, but in other ways she and I were mirrors of each other. Nearly the same height, though her heels were giving that illusion, same thin body type. I lacked her generous chest, but we shared high cheekbones, dark eyes, long hair.

I wondered if her desperation and terror had ever been reflected in my eyes. I guessed it probably had, the day I'd shown back up on my adopted family's doorstep. The first time I ran from Samir.

It broke my heart a little to turn and walk away. I opened the kitchen door, letting the cold October night sweep inside.

"I can't help you," I said. "You are a risk I can't afford. Go. Run."

She left without a word, leaving behind a silent room and the faint scent of blackberries.

I closed the door and leaned into it, listening to her footsteps retreat down the stairs. Only after I heard a car engine start and the crunch of tires on gravel did I turn and look at Alek.

"Did I just make a horrible mistake?" I asked.

"Perhaps," he said. "That was cruel."

"Geez, tell me how you really feel and totally don't hold back."

I unzipped my hoodie and hung it beside the door, then walked past Alek and into the bedroom. My limbs and heart felt like lead and I debated crashing without bothering with clothing or shoe removal. Alek had been sleeping over most nights, so we'd made a nest of quilts on the floor. It looked safe and inviting, if empty without a twelve-foot white tiger keeping watch over me.

Said tiger in human form came up behind me and pulled me into his arms. He tucked my head beneath his chin.

"It was cruel," he repeated. "But I understand. She is a dangerous unknown. There is too much at stake here, and we cannot trust her."

"The good of the many over the good of the one," I muttered. I felt shitty anyway. I had told her she was alone, on her own. She wasn't one of us, part of me and mine.

The safe decision, perhaps even the smart one. Definitely not the kind one. It was not what Sophie or Todd or Ji-hoon or Kayla would have done.

And look where it got them, the cold part of my heart whispered. *They are dead.*

I turned my face into Alek's chest and let my tears soak unnoticed into his shirt.

The next day was completely and almost suspiciously uneventful. I hung around my shop half expecting every person who walked through the door to be Tess, but none were. My friends were all busy with unicorn fever, taking turns watching over the recovering stallion. There was a minor argument over the name to give him, but common sense had prevailed and we all agreed on Lir, after the prince who had loved the last unicorn.

Depressing thought, really, in some ways. As far as Yosemite knew, Lir wasn't the last, but he might be the last in this wilderness. Unicorns were very rare, the druid said, and only thrived where the wilderness wasn't overly damaged. That was precious few places in the world anymore.

Harper called me two days after and said she was running late, so I opened the store by myself. Alek had gone with Yosemite into the woods that morning, leaving our makeshift bed in the wee hours with a soft kiss and assurance he wouldn't do anything stupid like get himself hurt or killed. I tried to pretend I believed him.

I was tidying up things that didn't really need tidying and avoiding doing translation work, which is what I do to actually pay the bills that comics and games don't cover, when Brie walked in. The tall baker was without her usual apron, but she had a box in her hands that smelled like sugar, spice, and everything buttery, fattening, and delicious.

It had been exactly a month since she'd told me in no uncertain terms that I wasn't allowed in her shop, that she wanted nothing to do with me, and that she considered me and my kind the epitome of all that was wrong with everything, ever. Well, those weren't her exact words, but she'd been pretty clear she meant it. I had been shocked and hadn't the heart to tell her that she paid rent to me every month, though for a second I'd been tempted.

"Don't give me a look like that," she said, setting the box down on the glass display counter that ran down one side of my store. "Iollan told me what you did. I admit I might have judged too harshly and too quick."

For a moment I couldn't figure out who Iollan was. "Yosemite?" I said.

She nodded, bright red curls bouncing with the motion, and looked down at the box. "I brought those little cupcakes you and Harper like."

"This mean I'm allowed to talk to you again?" I asked, raising my eyebrows. I really was trying to be civil, but her outright rejection of me had stung. But I really did miss those damn cupcakes.

"I knew a sorcerer once," she said, her eyes meeting mine. "He talked a woman I loved out of her home, away from family, hearth, and all who loved her. When he tired of her, he took her heart." Her eyes were shadowed with pain and she swallowed visibly.

"Sounds like we might know the same guy," I muttered.

"I guess we might," Brie said. "I do not like losing the ones I love. Ciaran assures me that you are different, but it is hard to trust."

I flinched inwardly at that. It *was* difficult to trust, and I was feeling the full consequences of that these last two days. I wanted to cast my eyes skyward and tell the universe that it was okay, I got the freaking message already.

"I'm glad I could help the unicorn," I said instead.

"I am also," she said. "He would not have let you help if you were of an evil disposition, I don't think."

Remembering that wild rush of power, the pure joy, I knew she was right. I tried to take some comfort in it.

"I am not sure I am very good," I said. I brought my hand to my mouth, surprised. Damn out-loud voice, sneaking up on me.

"None of us are only one thing or another," Brie said with a gentle smile that made her look strangely ancient and almost painfully beautiful from one breath to the next.

I wondered what she was, revising my idea she was just a hedge witch. I made a mental note to ask Ciaran when he got back from his latest antique-buying trip. Not that I expected a real answer from the leprechaun. He had a way of keeping secrets.

Brie had to get back to her bakery, and I resigned myself to waiting for Harper before I opened the cupcakes. Harper would never forgive me if I ate them without her and it wouldn't be worth the whining and reproach. Besides, she'd be shocked that Brie and I had made up. I couldn't wait to see her face when I told her. So I turned to my computer and opened the latest work file, making my brain move away from the world of unicorns and mysterious red-haired people with ancient

Irish names, and to Japanese car documentation contracts that needed to be put into English.

Harper's face was priceless when she showed up that afternoon and saw the box from Brie's bakery sitting on the counter.

"Did you check for traps?" she asked after I told her the story of my morning.

"Nope, I figured I would wait until the rogue got here."

"Maybe there's an invisible ooze or something," Harper said, poking at the box.

"Maybe it is poisoned. Should we call a cleric?" I sniffed the box, though I didn't really need to since the smell of sugar and lemon had been taunting me for hours now.

"Tell Max he can have my Game Boy," Harper said, pulling open the box and lifting a mini-cupcake out. She popped it into her mouth.

"It's a good day to die," I said, snagging a cupcake and following suit.

Harper replied but I couldn't make out a word of it around the mouthful of cake. Guess I'd finally found a language I didn't understand, har har.

"How's Lir?" I asked when we'd finished off all half-dozen cupcakes.

"He's standing, but still pretty weak. Max won't leave his side. It's kind of cute. But I get it, you know? I could almost like horses as much as he does if they all looked like a unicorn." Harper flopped into her usual chair and pulled her laptop from her backpack.

I almost told her about Tess, but she started humming and wasn't paying any attention to me at all, so I turned and went back to translation. The weather outside had turned blustery, and rain spat from the sky. It was a weekday, so there wasn't much traffic through the store. We worked in near silence, Harper playing *Hearthstone* and swearing about the RNG gods.

Possible conversational openers ran through my head. I wanted to share what had happened with her. She was my best friend. I trusted her more than anyone, maybe even more than Alek. I was afraid I'd made a horrible mistake with Tess, that I'd turned away someone in real need over stupid fears. I wasn't sure what I wanted Harper to say, how talking to her about it would assuage the guilt and doubt eating me alive, but it was getting messy to keep it inside. Part of not hiding anymore meant trusting the people around me with the ugly things as well as the good.

Besides, for all I knew, Harper would say good riddance, tell me in her best Mr. Torgue impression that Tess was going to betray the fuck out of me, and I'd find some kind of closure there.

"So," I said, "I had a visitor the other night."

Harper looked up from her game and tipped her head to one side. My face must have given away that this was serious because she slapped her laptop shut and set it on the counter beside where my phone was charging.

My phone buzzed, choosing the worst time, of course. I checked the text and saw it was from Alek.

"What's the word?" Harper asked.

"Nothing. He and Yosemite are doubling back; he says the trail keeps going in circles." I closed my phone after checking the battery level. I'd bought a cheap one this time, having lost the last two in pretty quick succession.

"So, someone came to see you?" Harper said.

The bell chimed as a figure pushed through the front door. This business would be so great if it weren't for the customers and their immaculate sense of timing, right?

Only it wasn't a customer. It was a bloody witch. Well, not literally bloody. Not yet.

"Hello, Peggy," I said to the head of the Wylde coven, putting a bit of frosty power into my tone so that my breath literally puffed with chill. I wasn't above theatrics, even if I couldn't turn her into a toad. Not yet, anyway, not before I heard her out. It would be impolite.

"Today is the thirtieth day," she said, no preamble, no pleasantries. Her hair was in its perfect bun, though damp from the rain, and she held a dripping umbrella in one hand which she pointed dramatically at me. "You are to be gone from this town by dawn, or else."

"Oh, for fuck's sake," Harper said. "Ms. Olsen, you are a total asshole, you know that?"

"Out of respect for your mother, young woman, I will ignore that you run with such a crowd and spare you."

"Spare me what?" Harper said, coming around the counter. "Plagues of bugs? Snootily looking down your nose at me? You are a fraud, all of you stupid witches. Jade could fry you like hotcakes into dust with a wiggle of her little finger, you dumb bitch. But you know she won't, which is why you feel okay threatening her, right? Cause you wouldn't be so goddamn stupid if she were actually dangerous."

Wow. I sat back, forgetting to be mad for a moment. I'd never seen Harper go after anyone like that, not even in the infamous flame wars on the net that she often found herself immersed in. I had to admit I was impressed and more than a little warmed by her profanity-laden defense and display of friendship. I prepared a shield, holding my magic tightly, my hands loose on my thighs, just in case Peggy the librarian got frisky when challenged.

Harper's jeans pocket began playing "The Imperial March" at the same time as my phone rang with "Bad to the Bone." It sounded like Max was calling his sister at the same time Levi was calling me. That couldn't be good. I froze, unable to decide between going for the phone and dealing with the witch.

"I will not be spoken to like this. You will rue this day, both of you." Peggy stuck her nose in the air in a bad high school drama way and shook her umbrella. "Hexen!" she shouted. The lights, my phone, both computers, and, judging from Harper's sudden leap sideways and subsequent outpouring of swearing, Harper's phone all flickered, crackled in spectacular sparks, and died.

Peggy fled as soon as it happened, making a very undignified exit out my door as quickly as she could.

I had no time to get a shield up, distracted by the ringing phones and more expecting an attack directly on Harper or me, not our poor innocent electronics. Summoning light into my d20 talisman, I held it aloft and surveyed the damage. The bulbs in my strategically placed lamps had all turned smoky black. Greenish, acidic smoke trailed off both computers. My phone was a useless brick of plastic. Light still shone from the street lamps and the bakery, so I had hope the hex hadn't damaged anything outside this room.

"She fried Cecilia!" Harper cradled her laptop in her arm, blowing at the smoke.

"I really hate witches," I said.

"We could go after her," Harper offered.

"Nope," I said. "We can't. One, she's probably in a car halfway across town by now, and two, you were right. I can't do shit about this without looking like a total asshole."

"I'm revising my opinion on that. This is, like, totally the gauntlet thrown, dude. So not cool." She opened her laptop and tried to turn it on, but we both knew it was a doomed act. "You would think she'd obey that threefold law thing. Bitch."

"Threefold law thing?" I asked.

"Yeah, I read it in one of the Wiccan books at the library. Supposedly if you do magic, it comes back to you three-fold, especially the bad stuff. So like you are supposed to avoid cursing people and crap, cause it'll just go like mega worse for you. Haven't you ever seen *The Craft*?"

"Guess I missed that one," I said. Wheels in my brain started turning as an idea began to form, as ephemeral as the dissipating smoke from my dead computer. "We should figure out why the guys were calling us, and then you can tell me more."

We never got the chance to do either. Brie rushed through the door into the mostly dark shop, cell phone in hand.

"They are under attack," she said. "We have to get to the Henhouse."

Clinging to the oh-shit handle in Harper's car as we barreled down the road toward the Henhouse, I finally understood the phrase "hell for leather." Brie was crammed into the back seat behind me, hanging on as well. All she knew was that Rosie had called her, saying there were demons trying to get to the unicorn, and telling her to go find me.

Harper pulled a turn worthy of an action movie as we hit the driveway for the B&B and bounced down the slick gravel driveway. The floodlights were ablaze around the paddocks and barn as we pulled up. The barn doors were closed, but the hayloft door was wide open, figures backlit against it. As I sprang out of the car before the engine had even died, I heard the panicked scream of horses followed by the crack of a rifle.

Rosie and Junebug stood side by side in the open doorway of the loft, rifles in hand, shooting into the seething mass of bodies around the paddocks. Max, in his wolf shape, and Levi, in wolverine shape, guarded the barn doors from the demons. I couldn't see Ezee.

"Demon dogs" was a more accurate description. The creatures were about the size of Great Danes, but heavier, with muscles that bulged beneath mottled grey skin. They had single eyes in the middle of their thick heads and single horns curving out between ratty, floppy ears. The horn was nothing like the unicorn's, more like an elongated rhino horn, pitch black in color and shiny as though wet, glinting in the light from the barn. Long, spikelike teeth gleamed in their widely gaping mouths and their claws would've made a velociraptor feel inadequate.

In other words, the demons were ugly and scary as hell.

I charged right toward them, trying to count as I went, magic singing in my veins as I threw a bolt of force into one demon, drawing the attention of three others who peeled away from trying to approach the barn door and charged at me. The bolt sizzled with purple fire as it threw the dog off its feet, but the creature rolled with the blow and joined its buddies in charging me.

Time for more firepower.

A large red fox streaked past me, snapping at a dog as she went, distracting the creatures from their charge as she flew by them.

"Harper," I yelled. "Reflex save."

She understood, and dodged at a ninety-degree angle, using her superior speed and smaller size to advantage.

I threw the fireball, pushing every frustrated, pent-up bit of anger I had into it. Which was a lot, apparently. I couldn't fry the annoying witches, I couldn't take back sending Tess away and being a terrible person, but damnit, I could throw down some serious burning pain on these reeking, evil monsters. It was nice to have something I could fight. Finally.

The ball of fire blew into the middle of the charging pack, changing growls and snarls to screams of pain as the dogs split in different directions. Two in the middle collapsed, burning and writhing. I cleared a path to my friends in front of the bar with a second fireball, trying to keep the range and size tight. Brie sprinted up beside me, a freaking long sword in her hands that blazed with white fire. I gawked as she twisted and spun, stabbing one of the dogs through its eye.

"Go for the eye," she gasped as we ran.

I did just that as another ugly monster sprang at me. I was too close to the barn now to risk another fireball. I aimed at it with a bolt of purple force. My bolt slammed into that red, evil eye, and the monster fell, not even twitching as it died.

"Go for the eyes, Boo!" I yelled, euphoric with the power running through me as I reached my friends.

Putting the barn door to my back, I surveyed the battlefield. The stalls were closed off from the paddocks by heavy metal doors, unlike the more decorative wooden door behind me. Junebug and Rosie were doing a good job of shooting the eyes out of anything that came over the fence into the small space of the paddocks. The demon dogs seemed intent on getting into the barn, but the women with rifles and the steel doors helped create a funnel toward Levi, Max, and now Brie, Harper, and myself. The pack decided the bodies looked easier to go through than the metal, but they hung back now, gathering in a dark half-circle at the edge of the light. More bodies were visible in the treeline.

"How many of them are there?" I asked, throwing another bolt at another glowing red eye. My bolts weren't quite quick enough at this distance and the monster dodged it with preternatural speed.

Beside me, Levi shifted to human, his breathing ragged and his lips still peeled back from his teeth in a snarl.

"At least two dozen," he said. "They got one of the horses, and Ezee is injured. He's inside. And he'll be okay," he added as I glanced at him, concerned.

"The fuck are these things?" I said.

"Fomoire hounds," Brie answered. "Creatures of filth and evil. They are here to finish the unicorn, I think." Her hair had come loose and spilled in deep red waves down her back and over her shoulders and her green eyes glowed as though lit from within. I'd never seen anyone look so badass in a flour-dusted apron before.

"Great, so we kill them." I rolled my shoulders, gathering more magic. I knew it was partially the adrenaline, but I felt ready to take on a couple dozen uglies. The air was filled with the scent of churned earth, gunsmoke, and burning flesh. An undercurrent of rot teased at my nose and I snorted, pushing it all away.

The uglies charged, this time with their heads down, horns in front. This made it hard to pick out eyes, but easier to fireball. I was glad for the recent rains as I threw a small orb of flame that expanded and grew with my will and power as it zipped over the ground to smash into the monsters.

At least three went down in flames, but more filled in to take their place. They moved across the open ground between the woods and the barn in a roiling black wave. My euphoria died down as I realized how many there were, but I pulled on more magic, willing another ball of fire into my outstretched hands, determined to take as many down as I could before they reached us. No way were these things going to finish Lir. I hadn't saved the unicorn just to let him die.

My next fireball was the last I could manage as the first line of hounds reached us. Wolverine-Levi barreled into one, his powerful jaws snapping its leg. Brie waded into the fray, her blade a white-hot streak as it sliced through grey flesh and slashed across red eyes. I refocused my magic, visualizing it as a beam of searing light, one hand now clutching my talisman as I dragged on more and more power, ignoring the sweat pouring into my eyes.

Purple fire streamed from my hand in a thin line, cutting into the eye of a hound as it tried to snap at and then gore the quick red fox leaping past. Harper didn't try to inflict much damage, just kept dodging and distracting, her sharp teeth snapping at tendons. Wolverine-Levi screamed in pain as one hound got its claws into him and I smashed my light beam into the monster, clearing it off my friend.

Levi scrambled back beside me, snarling. His shoulder was scored with bleeding claw-marks.

"Keep back," I hissed at him as I passed my beam across two more hounds, forcing them to retreat.

He shook his bearlike head and his muscles bunched as he prepared to leap once more into the fray. Harper and Max took down another hound between them, tearing into its hamstrings and flank, and Brie was a killing machine with her sword, but it seemed for every hound we felled, two came to take its place. We were hemmed in on three sides and I was running low on juice.

My head throbbed and I lost concentration, barely managing to avoid a black horn as it swept toward me. I sprang back, my shoulders slamming into the barn door, and threw my hands out, shoving magic at the creature with very little thought beyond "get it away from me."

The hound went flying backward like a boulder hurled by a giant, tumbling through the ranks of its companions. The effort left me weak and red dots swam in my vision. I had spent too much power, too quickly.

The hounds retreated for a moment, the ones I'd knocked down climbing to their feet. They closed ranks, still at least a dozen or more of them left, and stalked toward us, walking over the smoldering and whimpering bodies of their fallen kin. Beside me, wolverine-Levi crouched, shoulder still welling with blood. Harper and Max faced toward our open left side while Brie, her apron covered more in gore than flour now, faced slightly right, her sword still blazing, but her breathing audible and strained.

Even the horses in the barn were quiet now, and the rifles had stopped firing. I hoped that Junebug and Rosie were all right, but couldn't risk trying to look up and see.

One of the hounds in the front of the regrouping pack died to a rifle shot and I sagged in relief. They were still up there, and still had ammo. It was something.

We straightened up, ready for the next assault. The last assault. I wasn't so sure if we didn't take them out now that we'd be able to survive another wave. I shoved that sobering and awful thought away and dragged on the last reserves of my magic, feeling like I was scouring a soup bowl with my fingers for leftovers. Feeling like I *was* the soup bowl.

Beyond the hounds, the trees started to shake. Eerie howls picked up and the hounds seemed strengthened by it. A fresh wave of bodies burst forth from the trees, howling in greeting to their companions. Once again we were outnumbered by way too many to one.

"Fuck my life," I muttered. I had to manage at least two more fireballs for us to even stand a chance. It would probably knock me unconscious, but I had to try.

As I gathered power into my hands, bright green light poured out of the forest, and I realized the new hounds hadn't been howling in greeting, but in warning.

You haven't lived until you've seen a red-haired giant wielding a cudgel burst forth from a huge old oak tree on the back of a twelve-foot white tiger. Trust me.

Yosemite sprang from tiger-Alek's back in a cinematic leap worthy of Legolas and smashed apart the skull of a hound, his cudgel crushing through horn and bone as though they were rotten wood. Tiger-Alek's massive jaws ripped a monster's head clear from its body. One his huge paws, claws extended like a fistfull of katanas, swept aside another monster.

Brie cried out something in Old Irish and charged the pack. I threw my last fireball, the energy crackling out from my hands and fizzling pathetically into the front rank of creatures, doing not much more than singeing skin and angering them. Bending, I yanked Samir's dagger free from its ankle sheath and pushed what little power I could still summon into a half-shield in front of me. I knew the dagger was powerful, but it had come from Samir, and I was loath to use it. Desperate times, desperate measures and all that jazz.

Yosemite smashed another hound and started yelling, his voice booming across the field as he chanted. Vines and roots exploded from the grass, snatching at the hounds and dragging them down. The ones that ran for the trees found branches that lashed out, the forest around the barn beating any monster that came in reach to death with whomping blows as saplings bent and snapped in their fury.

Wolverine-Levi and I found ourselves fighting side by side again, keeping the barn as much to our backs as we could as three of the hounds decided we looked like less trouble than the bellowing giant, the woman with the flaming sword, or the dire tiger. I slashed with the dagger, painfully aware I had little idea how to fight without magic. My shield held, sparking purple as a hound slammed into it. Pain lanced up my leg as I barely dodged a clawed swipe. I prayed it was only a fleshwound and stumbled back.

My stumble left Levi's side open and a hound sprang in past me, horn aimed right at the wolverine's unprotected side. He twisted, trying to avoid the blow and a second hound's jaws closed on his leg with a sickening crunch. Levi went down and the first hound sprang onto him, its jaws wide and aimed at my friend's unprotected head. I screamed and threw my shield as though it were a physical thing, trying to turn the killing jaws aside.

Time seemed to slow, then scramble, then speed up again, as my vision stuttered and a blast of air took me almost off my feet. It was as though reality had become a faulty VHS tape recording.

Instead of closing on Levi's head, the hound's jaws snapped shut on Tess's abdomen as she materialized between the wolverine and the hound. She buried a large hunting knife in its burning red eye with a scream.

Adrenaline and power flowed into me, and I threw the dead hound off Tess and Levi. Levi struggled to rise, but Tess collapsed, blood spurting from the gaping wound in her stomach. The second hound sprang for Tess, and I threw every last shred of magic inside me at it.

"NO!" My voice was raw, the word clawing its way from my throat with the roar of blood my ears.

The hound exploded. Chunks of fetid, warm flesh rained down on me as I stumbled to Tess's side and crouched there, holding the dagger, waiting for the next attack.

It didn't come. The hounds broke and ran, tiger-Alek and Max giving chase as far as the glowing woods. It sounded from the shrieks that the trees did the rest of the killing work. I dropped Samir's dagger and yanked off my filthy teeshirt, pressing it to Tess's stomach.

"I'll live," she whispered.

"I know," I said. "Because you are a motherfucking sorceress, and so am I."

I held her gaze, willing her to stay with me as people came up around us, talking. My head swam in a lake of pain, and darkness pressed in on the sides of my vision. I was vaguely aware of Alek and Yosemite moving up beside me. I let them transfer Tess to a horse blanket and convey her to the house, reluctantly letting go of the blood-soaked teeshirt.

Harper slid herself under one of my arms, and I was surprised that Vivian, the vet, appeared and inserted herself under the other. She had a hunting rifle slung over one shoulder and a grim look on her face. I thought she said something to me, but my brain wasn't up for processing language anymore. Barely conscious, I managed to stumble with their help up to the house. I looked around as we went, making sure I saw each friend. Ezee, in human form, was limping with his twin, who was also back in human form. It wasn't clear who was holding up whom, but they were breathing, conscious, and alive. I didn't see Max until I looked back and caught sight of movement up in the hayloft. Max waved tiredly to me from his perch. Behind him, I could just barely make out Brie's figure, now holding a rifle instead of a sword.

Rosie and Junebug were on the porch, blankets in hand as we climbed the steps. Rosie said something to Harper and then darkness ate my brain.

I woke up on the couch in the main living room of the Henhouse to the soft murmur of voices and the smell of vanilla and spice. I was wrapped in a quilt with my head resting on a warm, muscled thigh. I knew that thigh, that warm energy, that scent. Alek.

"Hey," I said, struggling to unwrap myself as I turned my head and looked up at him, squinting into the light from the lamp beyond his shoulder.

"You all right?" he asked. He helped me sit up.

"Yeah." If I hadn't been, the concern and love emanating from his ice-blue eyes would have fixed any ill, I was sure. I poked at the yellow-green bruise and thin pink line on my leg which was all that remained of where the Fomoire hound had slashed at me.

"Good to see you again, Jade," said a rough, almost gravelly male voice and I looked over to see Aurelio, the alpha of the Bitterroot pack, sitting cross-legged on the floor. His shaggy black hair with its shock of bright white was loose over his bare shoulders and I swear he was wearing the same green sweats I'd last seen him in, a month earlier.

"Wish we could meet when things aren't trying to kill us, eh?" I said. "I thought you were leaving the area."

"I tried," Aurelio said with a grim smile. "Seems my pack is still needed. The forest is unquiet."

I looked around the living room. Judging from how healed my wound was, I'd been out at an hour or so. Max was wrapped in a quilt similar to the one around my almost naked torso and fast asleep in one of the oversize chairs. Harper and Rosie sat at the dining room table, their heads together as they spoke in voices too low for me to understand.

"Ezee is with Levi and Junebug upstairs," Alek said. "They are hurt, but nothing a few days of rest and Rosie's cooking can't cure."

Memories flooded back and I stared down at the dried blood rimming my fingernails. "Tess?" She was a sorceress, like me. She'd live through a wound like that, but it wouldn't be fun.

Alek jerked his chin toward the hall and the room where Harper had convalesced last month after nearly being turned into furry BBQ by Haruki the assassin. "Vivian is with her, seeing what she can do to get the bleeding to stop and close the wound."

"She'll heal, like I always do," I said. I stood up, wrapping the quilt around my body like a towel and tucking in the corner, since I had nothing but my bra covering my chest. Alek caught my hand and raised a pale eyebrow at me.

"I'm getting some water," I said. "And maybe finding a shirt."

I walked to the kitchen, not wanting to go see Tess yet. She'd come back. Part of me was relieved, in no small part because she'd probably saved Levi's life by appearing when she had. Part of me was afraid.

It was no coincidence that all this was happening now. I couldn't afford to be that naïve or optimistic. She'd shown up at precisely the right time, hadn't she? I hated myself a bit for being so suspicious. I clenched my hands into fists and went to wash her damn blood off them.

Harper and Rosie both looked at me but I shook my head in a "later" gesture and they let me pass without conversation. The kitchen was occupied, however. Brie and Yosemite stood there, arguing in Old Irish, keeping their voices low, but clearly not so concerned that anyone would hear them. I paused in the doorway, but they did little more than glance my way before resuming their conversation. Ciaran must not have told them I spoke Irish, or if he had, they assumed he'd meant only the modern language, not all its iterations.

"You cannot come with us," Yosemite said. "Ciaran comes home tomorrow, but he will not be in time. I cannot wait. You know that. If you were to lose yourself without him there…" he trailed off.

"You need my help. The two of you alone are not powerful enough if it is what we fear," Brie said. "I cannot let you go into the woods alone, not again."

"Who will stay and protect the unicorn?" Yosemite countered.

"The pack is here, and the sorceress can handle herself."

I finished rinsing my hands and poured a glass of water, taking a sip, swishing, and spitting it out. I drained the cup and turned to face them both. Yosemite's dual-colored eyes were shadowed by dark circles and his thick shoulders were hunched. He looked more exhausted than I still felt, a tree ready to topple in the next stiff breeze.

Brie appeared different. There was no trace of exhaustion around her. Her green eyes were bright, her curls somehow bouncier, and her lips and skin practically dewy with health and youth. She looked ten years younger. Her apron was gone, replaced by a teeshirt that read "Frag the Weak," which I recognized as one of Harper's.

"I'll go with you," I said to Yosemite as they stopped talking and regarded me in turn. I'd already figured the second person Brie had meant was Alek, and I wasn't letting him run off into the wilderness without me again.

"You?" Brie snorted. "You can barely stand up."

"I'll be fine by morning," I said, mostly sure I wasn't lying. I was tired, but the worst of the exhaustion had passed and my magic was there and strong when I reached for it.

"Please, Brigit," Yosemite said in Old Irish. "Stay and wait for Ciaran."

Brigit? The way he said the name rang a bell in my head, but whatever thought it was ran off before I could grasp it. Whatever Brie was, she was no hearth witch.

"Fine," she said after a moment. "You better let nothing happen to him."

"I believe Iollan can look after himself," I said in Old Irish, enunciating the words. "Or perhaps you missed the fight I just witnessed."

"I miss very little. Something it would seem we have in common, Jade Crow," she said, her mood changing from pissy to grinning in the blink of an eye. "I will wait and keep watch while you sleep," she said to Yosemite. She walked out of the kitchen and toward the back door.

"Who is she?" I asked the druid. We both knew I really meant "what is she?"

"That is a long story, and not mine to tell," he said. "I must rest. We will leave at dawn, before the trail goes too cold." He moved to follow Brie, stripping his clothing as he went, his steps lumbering and pained.

I set down my glass. Hadn't expected a strip show. Who were these people?

"He's going to recharge," Ezee said behind me. "He'll sleep out under the sky tonight, his body in contact with the earth. Tomorrow morning when the sun rises, he will be ready to go off and be a big damn hero again."

I looked over at my friend. Ezee wore another borrowed shirt, this one just plain black with a power button symbol on it. His hair was pulled back from his tired face and still damp from a shower. His brown eyes closed for a moment as Yosemite, now stark naked, left through the back door and vanished into the night.

"So," I said. "You and the druid, eh? When did that happen?"

"It didn't," Ezee said. "I mean, it does, sometimes. It isn't serious; we just see each other when he's in town sometimes. Rarely."

"Methinks you doth protest too much."

"Funny," he said, waving a hand at me in a vague STFU gesture.

"Seriously," I said. "You two seem pretty close."

"A bird may love a fish, but where would they build a home together?" he quoted.

"You know, they get together and live happily ever after at the end of that movie," I said.

"What? What movie? I'm quoting *Fiddler on the Roof.*"

Ha, whoops. "I thought you were quoting *Ever After.* I'll take 'nerds mixing up references' for six hundred, Alex."

We smiled at each other. Our smiles didn't last. Too much had happened.

"You know about folklore and stuff, right?" I said. "Why is Fomoire familiar to me?"

"So you'll actually take 'white people's legends' for six hundred," Ezee said. "The Fomorians were the original people in Ireland, I think. Irish myth isn't exactly my area of expertise. They were bad folk, but of course the people who fought against them and destroyed them would say that."

We shared another, sadder smile. Try growing up Native American if you ever want a stark lesson in how the conquerors rewrite history and even myth to suit themselves.

"Yosemite said those demon things were Fomoire hounds. They seemed pretty damn evil to me," I said.

"I'll ask him tomorrow," Ezee said. "Who is the woman that Vivian is trying to patch up? Seemed like you knew her."

Shit. I knew I couldn't dodge this question forever. But maybe a little longer.

"How is Levi?" I asked, aware of how obvious my ploy was.

"He'll be fine, thanks in part to that woman showing up and saving his ass, apparently. So?"

"I'd better tell everyone at once," I said.

"Levi is asleep and Junebug won't leave his side, so the rest of us will have to do," Ezee said, following me into the living room.

Harper and Rosie had moved from the table to the second couch, probably trying to give those of us in the kitchen some privacy. Max was awake, sipping tea.

"Can I borrow a shirt?" I asked Harper.

She jumped up and ran upstairs, returning with a grey long-sleeved teeshirt that had Pikachu on it. Mistake on her part, because I wasn't sure I'd give this one back. It was one of my favorites of hers. I pulled it on and took up a spot on the couch next to Alek.

"The woman who showed up tonight," I said, motioning with one hand toward the room where Vivian and Tess were. "She's a sorceress, like me. Kind of exactly like me." I took a deep breath, searching for the words. "She ran away from Samir this week and came to me. Or so she says."

"Samir?" Aurelio asked.

"Psycho sorcerer ex-boyfriend," Harper supplied. "He's been fucking with Jade, trying to kill her for, like, years now."

"Why didn't you tell us she was in town?"

I glanced at Alek, but he only raised his eyebrows at me. This was my mess and while his arm came around my shoulders in silent support, he wasn't going to clean it up for me.

"Because I sent her away, or at least I tried to. I don't trust her. You think all this stuff is happening right when she shows up is a coincidence? This is more of Samir's stupid games."

"So she's here to kill you?" Ezee asked.

"I don't know," I said. "She said she wasn't, and Alek says she's telling the truth, but I just don't know. I can't take the chance. Things are dangerous enough."

"If she wanted to hurt you, she has one heck of a way of showing it," Rosie said. "I saw her appear like that, put herself right between that demon and Levi."

"She saved my brother's life," Ezee said. "He told me. And now she's half dead in that room, her guts everywhere, half her blood on the driveway. Pretty shit plan if she wanted to harm us, no?"

I hated their logic. I hated that I still felt so much suspicion. I hated that I had sent her away and she had come anyway, showed up in my moment of need and done something I had failed to do. Saved my friend.

Letting out my breath slowly, I pushed all the hate away. Maybe that was the problem. Too much hatred for Samir, too much pain, so much it was blinding me when it came to him, to anything he'd touched. Maybe it was time to try accepting Tess at her word, give her a chance.

"I know," I said. "I might be wrong. I'm going to talk to her, see what she knows. This isn't a coincidence."

"Maybe he's pissed that she ran," Harper said. "Could he be here? Summoning those things? They weren't natural."

A small thrill went through me, followed by a spike of dread. If he was here, I wasn't ready. But I didn't know if I would ever be ready.

"I don't know. I'm going to talk to her, when she's awake."

Vivian emerged from the room, stepping into the hallway and turning toward us as our worried gazes all fixed on her. She wiped a bloody hand over her forehead, leaving a pink smear.

"She wants to talk to Jade," she said. "Don't overtax her. She's healing, but it'll be a while and she needs rest."

Be a while? I raised my eyebrows at that. Vivian didn't know how fast sorceresses healed. Tess's wound would already be closing after an hour. She'd have a hell of a bruise by morning and probably be tired and slow for a day or two, but by week's end she would be right as rain with just an ugly fading mark to show for being nearly bitten in half.

I got up, and Alek followed me. Behind me I heard Rosie offering Vivian a room and a change of clothes.

Tess was in the bed, quilts pulled up to her chin. Her face was pale, her cheeks sunken hollows. She opened her eyes as we entered.

"So," I said. "We meet again."

I sent Alek out of the room after asking him, in Russian, to ward it off for sound. I didn't want the details of the conversation I was hoping to have to reach my friend's ears before I could digest whatever information Tess could give me. Alek looked as though he would protest, but in the end all he did was sigh, set the silvery ward that would soundproof the room, and then he left.

Tess watched me with tired eyes as I sat on the edge of the bed.

"How do you feel?" I asked.

"Like something ugly tried to bite me in half," she said, a ghost of a smile playing at her mouth. She was beautiful even with smeared makeup and exhausted circles under her eyes. The effect made her look delicate and ethereal.

"You followed me," I said, then winced. I should have said something like "thank you for saving my friend," but the words came out way wrong.

"I told you, I have nowhere to go. I thought maybe if I stayed I could help somehow, convince you I'm not going to kill you." Talking looked like it hurt her and she closed her eyes.

"Thank you," I managed to say. "You saved Levi. How did you move so quickly?"

"I wish I'd moved faster," she said. "It looked like you would be okay so I hung back. I'm sorry."

"But how did you do it?"

"Time," she said. She opened her eyes, seemed to have trouble focusing on my face, and closed them again. "My powers mostly revolve around manipulating time. I can slow time down or speed it up, sort of. It is very localized, but I can make myself quick or someone else slow. It's my specialty, like elemental magic is yours."

Elemental magic was my specialty? That was news to me. I was good at throwing around power, good with fire and ice, or just pure magical force. I could do a lot of other things, however, like shields, basic wards, finding things and people. Even breathing underwater now. I'd been trying lately to teach myself to fly, but it was difficult to wrap my head around the "whole defying gravity for long periods" thing, so I hadn't managed more than a few feet of gliding so far. Samir had always encouraged me to use as much power as possible, to do the flashy, showy stuff like using fire or turning water to ice. Elemental magic, now that I thought about it.

I had never brought up the DnD spells I'd practiced and learned to control my magic with. The book was a game for children and I had wanted Samir's approval, had wanted so badly for him to love me and respect me and see that I wasn't just any girl, that I was mature and worldly. I shook my head over how ignorant he had kept me. Hansel in the cage, being fed sweets until slaughter time.

Tess's breathing evened out as she seemed to lose consciousness. Feeling like a creep but doing it anyway, I gently pulled back the quilt and peeled up a corner of the huge gauze pad across her abdomen. The wound was ragged still, but not bleeding. The edges were pressed closed as best Vivian could manage without sutures. From the clear beads around edges of the wound, it looks like she might have used glue. I looked around the room and spied a half-used tube of Super Glue on the dresser.

"Making sure I'm really wounded," Tess said.

"Sorry," I muttered. I pressed the bandage back down as gently as I could. "Why aren't you healing faster?"

"I am too tired to speed up time around myself," she answered. "I'll start tomorrow. Even with that, it'll be a couple weeks before I'm whole again, at least. So I guess I'm not much threat now, huh." Her chuckle ended quickly in a grimace of pain.

Alek wasn't in the room to tell me if she spoke the truth or not, but I had a feeling she did. A week until she was whole. I would have healed that wound in a day or three at most. My ignorance settled on me like a cloak I hadn't realized the weight of until just now.

"So you can't use magic other than the time stuff? What about what you did to the necklace?" I asked, trying to get more information without seeming as stupid as I felt.

"I removed it by making myself be elsewhere in time for a moment and letting the necklace remain," she said, as though it were perfectly clear what she meant.

Okay. Yeah. Not helpful. I filed away what she'd said for later examination.

"I can do small things. Power is power, after all, but it does not want to flow in ways we are not naturally inclined," Tess continued. "Have you never tried to do something very different from what you are good at, and failed?" Her eyes were open again and she stared steadily at me, her gaze intense, serious.

I thought about the time I had tried to heal Alek. Healing is apparently super hard. "Sure," I said, trying to nod in what I hoped was a sage manner. "I can't heal for shit."

"Who healed your leg?" She looked at my thigh, where my jeans still sported a bloodstained hole.

Well, fucktoast. I couldn't dodge that question gracefully. "I did," I said. "I mean, it healed on its own."

"You left a scar on him, on his arm," Tess said. "It never healed. He hides it with illusion and sometimes even make-up. He doesn't know I have seen it."

I knew she meant Samir. "It never healed?" I asked, pushing back the tide of memory that came with her words. My last meeting with Samir. My doomed charge to try and kill him after my family had blown themselves up rather than be used to torment and trap me. I'd thrown so much power at him, but it was all a blur in my memory. Wolf had come, had bitten him, the only time I'd seen her affect the physical world like that.

Turning my head, I looked toward where Wolf lounged on the floor. I hadn't even realized she was here, but somehow in that moment I knew she was and that if I turned my head, she would be there. Life was getting weirder. My guardian perked up her ears and lifted her head. The slash of white down her chest where Samir had wounded her showed starkly against her pitch-black fur.

"That is why I came to you," Tess said. "You got away. You hurt him, hurt him so badly that even after decades it has not healed but remains puckered and red, as though freshly closed."

"I can't remember what I did," I said, which was partially true. He'd nearly killed me, and Wolf had dragged me away. I took a deep breath and got to the topic I was dreading. It had to be talked about, or I could never even start to trust her. "Do you have anything to do with what is going on? You show up in town, terrible things start happening in the woods. I don't believe in coincidence, Tess. I can't afford to."

"Not directly," she said. "I think I know who might, though. I think it is partly my fault. I'm so sorry." She shivered and I realized I'd left her half uncovered.

"Samir followed you here?" I asked, helping her pull the quilt back up to her chin.

"No, not him, I don't think. Clyde, his other apprentice."

"There's two of you?" Samir apparently had been busy.

She nodded. "Clyde has been with him for a while. He's awful. All of Samir's cruelty, none of his reserve or finesse. I would have killed him years ago if I could, but the idea of eating his heart makes me sick."

"You ever eaten someone's heart?" I asked. She seemed to know what it entailed, at least, which made me think she had.

"Only once," she said, her eyes leaving mine and staring off into the middle distance that was memory.

She did not elaborate, and I found myself unwilling to ask more. I knew firsthand what a weirdly intimate experience it was, having done it twice now. And I understood what she meant about not wanting to repeat it with someone she loathed. The first heart I had taken had been of a serial-killing warlock and his evil, sickening memories still gave me nightmares sometimes.

I asked her questions about Clyde and the picture she painted was a bad one. His specialty was in raising spirits, warping them and infusing them with his own cruel and twisted desires. It made me think of Not Afraid and Tess confirmed that as far as she knew, Clyde had been involved in that, though mostly she thought it was Samir's doing. She claimed she hadn't been, that Samir didn't seem to include or trust her as much as he did Clyde. Apparently she was pretending to be very young and inexperienced in the hopes that Samir would continue to believe her not worth harvesting yet. She was tiring quickly, I saw, and I decided the rest of my million questions could wait.

"One last thing, just in case," I said. "What does Clyde look like? What does his magic smell like?"

"Smell like?" she asked, her face a picture next to the word *confusion* in the dictionary.

"Magic has a smell, a feel, a taste. I don't know how to describe it," I said, waving my hands in the air. "Your's is cool, crisp, like a frosty morning."

She blinked up at me and her tongue flicked over her lips. "I cannot smell or taste someone else's magic," she said. "I can see the effects, see the obvious things like you throwing fire. I have never heard of anyone who can sense another without taking their power first."

I racked my brain. Surely this was something Samir and I had discussed. I couldn't remember it ever coming up and I wasn't willing to take a super in-depth trip down memory lane to find out if it was something he knew about me or not. "Huh," I said.

"Clyde is blond, looks mid-twenties, and is very pretty," she said, her eyes keen but her voice fading almost to a whisper with exhaustion. "He's a little taller than you, but almost as thin, and his voice is nasal, whining. He's also completely devoted to Samir and a total idiot about what Samir will do to him when he finally tires of Clyde."

"Thank you," I said. "Rest. I have to go away in the morning to help hunt down those hound things, but you'll be safe here, I think."

"I can stay?" she said and the hope in her face broke my heart all over again.

"Yes," I said, because I no longer had it in me to say no.

Max, Ezee, and Harper were arguing in the living room when I emerged.

"What? I'm totally Oona!" Harper said.

"I called dibs on Jack already. I mean, I totally helped save Lir, both times," said Max.

"I think that makes us Screwball and Brown Tom," Ezee said with a tired grin.

"So wait," I said, figuring out after a moment what the hell they were talking about. "I'm Lili, right? I look good in black."

"That would make me Jack," Alek said, rising from beside the door where he'd stationed himself and coming up behind me to wrap his arms around my waist. "But I'm far too tall and blond to play Tom Cruise."

"Wait, you showed him *Legend*?" Harper asked.

I looked up at Alek, impressed. "Nope," I said. "He got this reference all on his own."

"In Soviet Russia," Alek said, smiling down at me and playing up his accent, "references get you!"

When everyone had stopped dying of laughter and shock, we regrouped in the living room. Aurelio had left to check on his pack and Rosie had gone to bed.

"Is she staying?" Harper asked me.

"Tess? Yeah. I think so. I am going into the woods with Alek and Yosemite tomorrow. We might not be back for a couple days. If she tries anything, just cut her head off and stick it in the freezer and I'll deal with her when I get back."

"I'd laugh, but one, my sides hurt already, and two, I think you are like totally serious."

"Mostly," I said, smiling at my friend. "She's pretty damaged. Just… Be careful."

"We'll keep an eye on her for you," Ezee said. "But seems like she could use friends, too."

We gathered just after daybreak. Alek and I had made a
run to my apartment to collect things, like clean clothes,
sleeping bags, and my hiking boots. Yosemite said he had
a feeling where the hounds had come from, now that he'd
seen them, but it was going to be at least overnight to
hike out, maybe longer since we'd have to track the
survivors if we could and make sure they weren't
doubling back for more.

I described Clyde as best I could from what Tess had
told me and Aurelio said he would pass it on to his
wolves. Everyone was going to stay at the Henhouse. I'd
put the closed sign up on my shop, as had Brie. There'd
be some questions from regulars about it, but we'd deal
with those later, I figured.

Tess woke up long enough to promise me that Clyde would get to my friends only over her dead body. I still wasn't sure what to make of her yet, but from the grim approval in Alek's eye after she said this, I had to believe she meant it enough to pass his lie-detector senses. That was some comfort.

I walked out to check on Lir, the unicorn. One of Max's ponies had been mauled, a little grey named Merc, but Ezee had told us all about how the unicorn had touched his horn to the wounds and brought the pony back from the brink of death. The little gelding would have scars to show, I saw, running my fingers over the long pink lines, but he was alert and munching hay.

Lir greeted me with a huff of air and a gentle bump on my shoulder with his nose. I stroked his uber-soft fur.

"Lend us some luck, okay?" I murmured.

His intelligent dark eyes watched me in silence as I left the stall. He was magnificent, and my heart hurt looking at him, a tightness in my chest full of wonder and fear for his life. I wanted to kick even more Fomoire ass, and this Clyde guy, too.

Alek had been right. Killing did get easier, especially when the stakes were so high.

Yosemite explained what he thought might be happening and to my surprise he said that he'd spoken with Tess and she agreed it was in the realm of possibility for Clyde to do.

Apparently, back in the time of legend in Ireland, there'd been a really bad dude named Balor Birugderc, also called Balor of the Evil Eye. He'd led the Fomoire against the Tuatha Dé Danann and been slain by a guy named Lugh.

The part of the legend that hadn't made the books and retellings was that the head of Balor had been given to the first druid for safekeeping, and passed on through the ages until it fell to one of the last druids, a youth named Iollan, who, after a few centuries, emigrated from Ireland to what became the United States, and buried the head in a wilderness full of powerful nodes and unbroken ley lines.

Working theory was that Samir, and thus Clyde, had somehow learned this and figured out a way to peel back the lid of Balor's evil eye.

"Seven lids," Yosemite said as we hiked. "Balor's power is much reduced by his death, but it could still kill this whole area."

The forest we hiked through was in full autumn foliage, the deep greens of the evergreens mixing with red and gold from birch, maple, and oak. The ponderosa pine needles had turned to flame red, and fallen leaves created a thick carpet under our feet. Deer flashed tails at us as they took offense at our intrusion. We climbed elevation, the forest growing sparser. Many of the bushes and ferns had turned to red and gold as well, and the grasses between boulders and sheets of grey rock were yellowed. For hours we hiked mostly in silence, moving more slowly than the two of them might have without me. Occasionally Yosemite would pause and point out a wildflower, or a tiny squirrel. His love of the land radiated from him, showed in how he moved through the woods and over the open, rocky areas with ease and comfort.

Occasionally he would stop and confer with Alek about the trail we were following. I tried to pick out tracks, look for signs, but broken twigs looked like broken twigs to me, and the hounds hadn't left much. Yosemite and Alek agreed about which direction we should keep moving in, so I put my trust in them and tried to keep up.

I'm a nerd, I hang out in my store, I play video games. My idea of a workout was playing paintball for a couple of hours. I'd been getting in better shape over the last few months out of sheer self-defense, swimming, even lifting weights with Levi's coaching. Alek and I had started going for runs now that he was back. I still found myself breathing hard as the sun climbed, hit its zenith, and began to descend.

There was that whole "we could be attacked at any time" tension, too, which didn't help. I couldn't just relax and enjoy the nature walk. I kept looking around us, waiting for the proverbial killing shoe to drop.

Day moved to night and we set up camp on a wide stretch of open ground on a hill above a large creek. Two huge boulders had crashed together at some point in the last million years and created a wedge-shaped shelter. With rock on three sides, we felt safe enough camping, though we didn't risk a fire. Dinner was protein bars and water.

Alek slept in tiger form, eschewing a sleeping bag. I dragged myself into mine and curled up against his huge, furry side. I was used to sleeping next to a giant tiger at this point. There's something comforting about it, like knowing you have the biggest, baddest mofo in the room on your side, keeping watch over you. Even so, it took me a long time to get to sleep. I stared up at the stars, wondering where Samir was, worried about my friends back at the Henhouse. Eventually the physical exertion of the day won out and I faded into sleep.

The second day we crested a ridge and then began a slow, painstaking descent down shale-covered slopes toward a thick patch of forest below. The sky was overcast, but so far the day was mild for October and it hadn't rained on us. Even to my untrained eye, it was clear something was wrong with the land here. The leaves were off the trees and the trees themselves looked charred, as though from recent fire. The air smelled of smoke and wet charcoal. The grass was all dead—not the aged yellow it had been the day before, but a wet, unhealthy, slimy brown color.

"Was there a forest fire here?" I asked. "I don't remember that being on the news." Fires this late in the autumn would have been reported, especially one close to Wylde. We'd hiked all day, but I doubted we were more than twenty or thirty miles inside the wilderness area.

"No," Yosemite said. "This is worse than it was even days ago when I last came this way. I fear I am right about Balor's Eye."

We had hit the bottom of the valley, almost to the tree line, when movement caught my eye. I froze, turning toward the wide expanse of dying grass to my left.

The dead forest covered much of the valley floor and the far side, but there was nothing but open ground to our north. Shale and grass and brush spread out from the edge of the dying forest in a wide plateau. In the very edge of the distance I could see, a huge grey boulder stood up and shook itself with a roar that crackled in the dead trees and echoed down the valley and back with eerie reverberations.

Then the giant rock charged, shaking the ground as it moved. Moved straight at us.

9

Alek went from man to tiger in a blink beside me. Yosemite shouted at me to run for the trees, but he had his feet set like he was preparing for a fight, so I said fuck that and summoned magic, bracing myself as well.

The rock monster bounded closer. It looked like something dreamed up by the artists of *Shadow of the Colossus* only without the pretty green mossy bits or the shiny scrolly bits. Instead it had cracks between plates of grey stone that gleamed with dull red light. It was shaped like a rhino crossed with a turtle and a bit of insect thrown in, its six legs stumpy but apparently effective in moving its bulk. Its head was huge with thick horns protruding from the sides like a bull's and a round nose like the head of a hammer. If it had eyes, I couldn't make them out at this distance.

Distance that was quickly going away. Yosmite shouted in Old Irish and vines burst up from the ground, wrapping around the rock beast's legs. They might have been made of dental floss for all the care it took of them. The vines fell away, snapping like Silly String, with no effect.

"The earth here is too sick," Yosemite gasped out, sweating beading on his forehead. "It cannot fight properly."

"Maybe we should move," I said. I didn't think a fireball was going to do much to that thing. It definitely looked like it was made of rock.

"Trees," the druid said.

The three of us turned and bolted for the forest, but it was clear from the shaking of the ground that we weren't going to make it. I veered at a ninety-degree angle and dove painfully over a chunk of rock as the beast reached us, its huge head sweeping side to side as it reared back and tried to stomp on Alek. Tiger-Alek leapt for its face, knifelike claws extended. He didn't even scratch the surface, and the beast threw its head around until he was forced to leap free. He landed with a rolling skid and regained his feet, a deep roar coughing from him as he retreated and circled toward me.

I aimed bolts of force at the dull red cracks in the stone, hoping that would be a weak point. No dice. My bolts sizzled, fizzled, and did little more than attract the creature's attention. It bellowed again and backed off, pawing at the ground.

We ran for the trees again, putting distance between the beast and ourselves. The dead forest would provide little coverage, but little was better than none.

I stumbled into the treeline next to Yosemite and looked at the druid.

"How do we stop that thing?"

"I have no idea," he said. "Drop trees on it?"

"Can you do that?"

"In another part of the forest, perhaps. Here, there is not enough life to answer my call," he said, shaking his head. "This was one of the guards set long ago. But something is wrong with it. She will not heed my call; she is no longer tied to the land."

The beast shook itself and oriented toward us, pawing the earth, sending grass, topsoil, and chunks of shale flying. It was going to charge again.

"Like something out of a freaking anime," I muttered, trying to figure out how to stop it. Transmute rock to mud? It was an oldie but goodie from the Dungeons & Dragons spell book, but I wasn't sure I could pull it off, not without that thing holding still so I could concentrate. "Wish we could summon Goku." Never a Super Saiyan when you needed one.

Or was there? I stood up straighter as the beast pawed the earth again. Tess had said we had specialties, right? She thought mine was elemental magic, but I knew that wasn't really the case. I was best when it came to throwing around lots of raw power. I had been training all summer to gain more finesse, more control, to do more with less. Shoring up the areas I was weak more than trying to strengthen the things I was good at. Maybe I'd been going about it all wrong.

"Get behind me," I shouted as the ground shook and the beast charged.

I pulled power into myself, grabbing at every shred I could summon and hold without losing concentration. I slid my left foot forward and thrust my arms out behind me, focusing all that energy into a ball between my hands.

Yosemite and Alek moved, retreating further into the trees. Smart men.

The beast wasn't so smart. It crashed toward me like a wrecking ball. What happens when an irresistible force meets an immoveable object? I had no idea why that popped into my head, but I went with the thought, pouring every ounce of strength and belief in my own irresistible power. I waited until the stone beast was almost to me and then...

"KAMEHAMEHA," I screamed. I threw my hands in front of me, unleashing the beam of pure force right the beast's ugly face.

The beam exploded into the beast, lifting it completely off its feet and rolling it up like a potato bug before flinging it back along the ground like an out-of-control, off-balance bowling ball. I had to turn my head away from the sudden gritty wind that erupted as debris flew into the air in its path.

Rubbing my eyes with my shirtsleeve, I peered out of the trees and down the deep furrow the rolling beast had left. It lay, unmoving, about two hundred yards away, half buried in the side of the valley. I reached for more power and stumbled toward it.

Up close it smelled like ash and rot. The beast wasn't dead, its side rose and fell very slowly, but its chest was caved in and rust-colored ichor leaked out, too thick to look like proper blood. I really didn't want to touch it, but I couldn't have pulled off another giant spell if my life had depended on it.

Gripping my d20 for focus, I pictured what I wanted to do, and laid my hand on its bulbous nose. The beast snorted, dull red nostrils opening and closing as fetid smoke gushed forth. I choked and hacked as my eyes watered, but kept my hand where it was.

Rock to mud. I couldn't remember all the details of the spell, though I knew there was something in there about not working on magical stone. Fuck that, because the manual wasn't a spell book, not in reality. In reality, I just needed to have the power and the belief I could do it.

At that moment, I believed I could do anything. I'd just cast Kamehameha, or Turtle Devastation Wave, as translated from the Japanese. It had seemed appropriate, given the way this beast looked. Super effective, if utterly exhausting.

I pressed power down into its rocky skin through my hand. The magic animating it was inky and black, just like the corruption I'd burned out of the unicorn. Clyde, if I had to guess. My power sank in and the stone bent to my will, softening, cracking, turning to black, sludgy mud and finally splitting and sliding away in huge chunks. Rust-colored smoke gushed from the melting head and I held my breath, keeping my magic sinking into the sludge beneath my palm until the creature stopped breathing.

Stumbling back, I spat to try to clear the filth from my mouth, and then gasped in mostly fresh air. Alek, back in human form, was there to catch me as I collapsed. This time, I didn't even resist as he lifted me into his arms. I buried my head in his chest and let exhaustion take me away.

I came awake tucked against Alek's side. It was nearly dark, the moon rising above the rim of the valley. He'd brought me back up to the top and we were tucked against a large rock.

"Didn't want to camp down in the valley of death?" I asked.

"Not safe," Alek said. "How are you feeling?"

"Like I just stopped a freight train with my face," I said. My mouth tasted of smoke and sour beer and my eyes were gritty when I rubbed them. I took the water Alek offered and tried to drink slowly.

"Where's the druid?" I asked, looking around.

"Valley," Alek said. "He went to check on the head."

"Hope there aren't any more of those stone turtle things."

"He says there are two others."

"Great," I muttered. "Can we fight them tomorrow? Because I don't think I can do that twice."

Alek's smile flashed white in the gloom. "Whatever that was, it was impressive."

This was what I got for falling for a non-nerd. Harper or Levi or Ezee would have been gushing with glee over what I had done. They'd be talking about it for months. I just hoped they'd believe me, but there was no way it would be as cool when I told it as it would have been if they had witnessed it, damnit.

"Gee, thanks," I said, knowing he'd see my eye-roll with his much better low-light vision. "We got any more of those power bars left?"

Yosemite returned sometime in the night, long after I'd drifted back to sleep. I awoke with the sun and he was there, wide awake, watching the sun rise over the ridge. The air was cool, and the wilderness quiet as a grave. No morning birds sang.

"What's the story?" I asked the druid.

"I cannot get to Balor's head. There are two more guardians in the way, camping directly over the burial mound, plus I sense a pack of Fomoire hounds nearby and coming closer. I am not sure it would matter, in any case. I cannot close the lids." He rubbed his hand over his face, looking older and utterly tired.

"So we gather up the gang, bring as much firepower as we can muster, and come lay down the hurt," I said. I was not looking forward to fighting two more of those rock monsters, or another pack of hounds, but what choice did we have? I hoped that with Tess's help, maybe I could track Clyde and put a stop to his shit as well.

Of course, I might not have to. If I ruined his little Balor party, he would probably come to me. I was his end goal, after all.

"Did you not hear me?" Yosemite said. "I cannot close the lids. I cannot purge the land. It is too late—even if we stop this sorcerer polluting and twisting the spirits of the forest, I do not have the knowledge to close the eye."

"Who does?" I asked. "I mean, the druids gave you this head but didn't teach you how to stop it if something happened?"

"Jade," Alek said softly in that tone he used when I was being a bitch.

Yosemite waved his hand in an "it's okay" gesture, quieting Alek.

"There is a ritual. There were once many rituals, most lost to time now. But some, the most important, were written down by the druid who trained me. He had three copies of the book made. So far as I know, only one has survived the centuries."

"Great," I said. "So we can do the ritual and stop this. Where is the book? Ireland? Buried inside a glass mountain and guarded by a fox with nine tails? I'm up for a quest." I smiled at him, trying to bring some lightness to his grim, unhappy face.

I failed.

"Seattle," he said. "But it doesn't matter. I cannot read it."

"Seattle?" That was only an eight-hour drive away. "Why can't you read it?"

"My teacher wrote it in an ancient script, known only to a few. He meant to teach me the letters, but he was killed before he had a chance. His knowledge died with him, for he was the last who knew the secret tongue."

"Okay, let me get this right. There is a ritual in a book in Seattle that can close Balor's Eye and stop this?"

"Yes, and also I think a ritual that will wake the soul of the wilderness here and cleanse the land. But as I said, it doesn't matter." He got to his feet and turned away from us, his face lifting to catch the first rays of the morning sun. His cheeks above his thick red beard were suspiciously damp.

I looked at Alek and watched as comprehension dawned on his handsome face. He smiled, and I returned it, brushing my fingers over his. He squeezed my hand and then let go.

"So if you could read the ritual, or rituals, we could fix all this?" I got to my feet and waved my hand at the valley below.

Yosemite rounded on me and snorted in frustration. "Yes," he said. He closed his mouth on whatever he was about to follow that with, looking down into my smiling face.

"Cool," I said. "Because I can read any language. It's kind of my superpower."

"Any language?" He blinked at me.

"Yep, so far as I know." I could tell he was skeptical, so I took a deep breath. I wasn't fond of talking about Samir, but it was getting slowly easier to share. "It's how I found out my psycho ex was going to kill me. He keeps journals, written in a mix of dead languages and some words he's made up all on his own, I think. He believed that no one could ever decipher them. He was wrong. So I'm pretty sure I could read your book."

Yosemite pursed his lips and folded his arms. After a long moment he nodded. "What have we to lose?" he said.

Howling broke the morning silence. It sounded distant, but not distant enough for my taste. I started stuffing my sleeping bag into its sack as quick as I could. Alek rose to his feet, sniffing at the air.

"Let's get out of here," he said. "They are closer than they are letting on."

"We shall find healthy trees," Yosemite said. "Then I can open the leaf-way to get us back to the Henhouse."

"Not that again," Alek said with a grimace.

"We can't waste another day, not when we must travel to Seattle and lose time already. The forest sickens; the land will die permanently if we delay too long. We must move with haste now."

"Tree travel it is," Alek said with a resigned sigh.

"How bad can it be?" I asked as we took off over the ridge. Famous last words, right?

The uneven ground had entered into a conspiracy to slow me down, trip me up, and make me dog food. Swear to the universe. I was never going hiking again. We raced over the ridge and down the other side, Yosemite and Alek leaping and gliding over rocks and brambles toward the line of healthier forest far below and beyond us. All those hours climbing up this ridge to get to the valley, all that effort, and now I had to stumble my way down at breakneck speed. I would have sighed, but I had no breath to spare.

Breakneck speed was an accurate phrase for it. I gave up after the second fall ripped my jeans open at the knees and embedded thistle needles into my palms. I reached for my magic, letting it run through my muscles, strengthening me, lifting me up as I sprang a few feet off the ground and forward, leaping like a long-jumper. Using my magic, I pressed down, willing myself not to land, but to keep going. I'd learned in my AP Physics class in high school that gravity is considered a weak force and I intended to ignore the shit out of it for as long as I could if it meant not face-planting again before reaching those trees.

Even with magic, I could barely keep up with Alek and Yosemite, their long legs eating up the distance, their huge bodies apparently good enough at defying pesky things like air resistance and gravity all on their own.

Behind me, the baying of the Fomoire hounds grew louder, closer. I couldn't risk a look, but it felt as though they were closing the distance, definitely over the ridge themselves by now. I wanted to turn and tear into them, but memory of our barely won fight at the barn kept me gliding forward, kicking off the ground for another long glide. All I needed was a Hidden Leaf headband or an Anbu mask and I'd be right at home in a *Naruto* manga.

The healthy forest spread out ahead of me, the leaves looking like they were on fire in the morning sunlight, lit from the side by the rising sun. We were nearly in its shade when the first of the hounds caught up.

Fetid and heavy breathing warned me, and I threw myself sideways, using my magic like a ski pole to shove my gliding body aside as a hound sprang at me from behind. I shouted a warning as I hit the ground, the impact jarring me from ankle to teeth. I managed to keep my feet and spin, lashing out with a beam of purple fire. The hound dodged and went for Alek instead.

Alek shifted and sprang, his huge jaws ripping into flesh with satisfying crunches, paws bigger than my head with claws longer than my fingers tearing the hound to whimpering shreds.

Yosemite had reached the trees, and he turned as well, a thick branch, its length still covered in twigs and leaves, dropping from the trees to his hand. He spun it with mastery, cracking into one monster's skull and spinning back to trip another and send it flying into the trees. Vines ripped up from the ground, glowing green in the dim light beneath the trees. Any hound that shot past us was caught, yowling in pain, and dragged into the earth.

The pack backed off as a high whistle sounded and the ground shook. There were less of them than before, I noticed as I edged toward Alek and the druid, gasping for air. Still too many; twenty or so at least. I raised my eyes as Yosemite cursed in three different tongues and looked back up the hill.

One of the stone turtle insect guardians, its craggy body oozing rusty smoke, lumbered down the hill. It wasn't moving very quickly, but it was picking up steam as it went. The one the day before had moved better, and after a moment I could make out why this one was more cautious.

It had a rider. A man stood on its back, his golden hair bright, a motherfucking crimson cloak streaming out behind him.

"Fucking theatrics," I muttered.

"That the sorcerer?" Yosemite asked. He had half turned away and was looking at the trees around us as though searching for something.

"A sorcerer," I said. "Not Samir. I think that's Clyde."

I set my feet, one back, one front, and started to pool magic into my hands, balling force as I had before. Bowling that stupid turtle down would be even more satisfying with that clown on its back. He was an idiot to come out in the open. I smiled.

Just a little closer, fuckwad, I thought, watching Clyde come down the hill. I could make out his features now. Delicately pretty, like Tess had said. He was grinning fit to split his face. Well, that made two of us.

"Jade," Yosemite hissed, his voice filled with fear and urgency. "The other guardian, it's behind us."

I risked a glance behind, clinging to my focus, holding the gathering ball of magic in my hands. Something grey and black slithered between the trees, brush crackling as it came closer. I made out a snakelike head and rust-colored eyes or maybe nostrils, smoking beneath the trees.

"I don't think I can take out two, and the hounds," I hissed back.

"I can open the way, but only in that tree," Yosemite said, pointing toward an oak about twenty yards to our left. It was bigger than the trees around it, growing at the edge of the wood where it had gotten plenty of light and water.

Alek crouched by my side, growling low in his throat, his whole body vibrating with tension.

The stone turtle insect stopped its advance, and Clyde called out to me, "Good morning, Jade Crow."

Cocky cocksucker. My whole body shook from holding the spell. It wouldn't be as strong as yesterday's; my reserves were still low.

"Good morning, Clyde," I called. Then, in a whisper, I said in Old Irish, "Start going to the tree, I'll distract him," and added the words in Russian for Alek's benefit.

"I see our little traitor has been talking," Clyde yelled. "You think she won't betray you, like she did Samir?"

Something about his words bothered me, but I shoved them aside. I couldn't hold the spell much longer.

"Fuck off," I yelled. Out of the corner of my eye, I saw that Alek and Yosemite had halved the distance to the tree. It would have to be good enough.

"You are trapped," Clyde called out. He started to say something else stupid and gloaty, but I threw my hands forward, unleashing the Kamehameha.

The energy ball ripped along the ground, tossing hounds out of its path like sticks. It slammed into the polluted guardian, rocking the creature backward and bowling it off its feet in a cloud of dirt and shale.

I bolted toward the tree, not watching to see what further effect my spell had. The stone snake guardian rushed us, crushing ferns and saplings in its path as it abandoned stealth for speed.

Yosemite was chanting, green light streaming from his hands and into the oak. A glowing portal opened in the trunk and he half shoved tiger-Alek through it and reached for me as I made one last magic-assisted leap. The snake's jaws snapped just where I had been, its breath an ill wind at my back. I dove into the leaf-way.

There was no ground, no up or down. I flew through empty space, feeling like I was moving or that perhaps the filtered green light that danced all around me was moving and that I was just falling. Falling forever, my heart in my throat. If that was what skydiving was like, I made a solemn vow right then and there to never ever try it.

I clutched at my d20 talisman with both hands, needing something solid to remind me I was here and real. I was a sorceress. Hitting the ground after a fall like this wouldn't kill me. If there was ground. Hadn't Alek and Yosemite come out through the ancient oak at the Henhouse, safe and sound, only days before? I tried to cling to that memory, to the knowledge that whatever was happening would pass and I would survive it.

I slammed back into daylight, ground beneath my feet for a moment until my toes tripped me up as my forward momentum carried me into a full-on-face plant in the dewy grass outside the Henhouse. I almost kissed that ground as I realized I was here and it was solid, but I was afraid if I opened my mouth, I'd barf.

Alek, back in human form, leaned down beside me, helping me to my feet.

"How bad can it be?" he said, eyebrows raised.

"Okay, you win," I said, swallowing hard. "Let's never do that again."

Yosemite leapt from the tree behind us as though he'd been on a stroll, and turned, banishing the green light and closing the leaf-way. I really wished he'd said something cool, like "The way is closed" but you can't have everything, I guess. Besides, hadn't I just been disgusted with Clyde the evil sorcerer for being overly theatric? That was partially sour grapes on my part, I knew. His little distraction plan had almost worked, though I wanted to believe I could have taken him, and his little dogs too. All two dozen of them. And two giant monster things made of nearly impregnable stone.

Yeah, those grapes would have tasted like shit. The fox was so right.

We walked into the Henhouse after checking on Max and the unicorn. A few lights were on and I heard voices as I entered. The whole lower floor smelled of butter popcorn. The first person I saw was Harper, walking between the kitchen and the open door to Tess's room, a huge bowl of popcorn in her hands—which explained the scent at least. She looked tired but had a smile on her face that grew grim when she saw us.

"You guys are a mess," she said. "You okay?"

"Yeah," I said. "Everyone in Tess's room?"

It sounded that way, at least, their voices spilling out into the hall.

"I must make a phone call," Yosemite said. He went up the stairs without another word.

I followed Harper into Tess's room, Alek behind me. Levi, Ezee, and Junebug had all set up camp there, as far as I could tell. They'd brought one of the flatscreen TVs into the room and I recognized the closing credits from *Firefly* paused on the screen. Tess had more color in her cheeks, but still looked delicate and weak in the bed, propped up on half a dozen pillows.

"You guys been up all night?" I said.

"We were worried about you guys," Levi said.

"So we started watching Firefly," Ezee said, with a shrug.

"Next thing we knew, it was morning," Levi finished.

"You are just in time though," Tess said. "We finished the first season, but we haven't started season two yet."

"Season two?" I said, raising an eyebrow at the twins. "You didn't warn her?"

"We didn't have the heart," Harper muttered as she set the popcorn down on the nightstand.

"Warn me about what?" Tess asked, looking between their faces.

"There is no season two," I said, glaring at my friends. I felt like I was in some alternate universe. I went away for a few days and everyone was hanging out like old friends, turning our new friend into a *gorram* Browncoat while they were at it.

"What do you mean there is no season two?" She looked crushed. I knew the feeling.

"Fuck this," I said, throwing up my hands. "I'm going to go take a shower. You guys can explain things. Then we'd better tell you all what we found."

I left to the sounds of another fangirl heart breaking in twain.

It appeared that the Henhouse and surroundings had been quiet while we were gone, which was a relief. No one had tried to get to the unicorn again. If I had to guess, I would have put my money on Clyde being distracted hunting us through the woods, trying to catch up to us once he'd realized we were tracking the hounds and heading for Balor's burial site.

We wasted little time, despite being exhausted with almost no sleep. Clyde had no reason not to come after us, perhaps bringing the stone guardians with him this time. Yosemite thought we had a day, maybe a day and a half on them because of the tree travel. Ciaran, surprising me, showed up as I wolfed down an omelet. He and Brie would go into the woods, he said, and see what they could do to slow the pack's progress.

I tried to protest, of course, but he just looked at me with his ancient eyes and I shut up. All three of them, Brie, Yosemite, Ciaran, were a lot more than they seemed and I had to accept that I wasn't the only badass in the room. In some ways, it was a relief. I wasn't alone against Clyde and his filth.

I'd spent a lot of the last month feeling alone, despite my reconciliation with Alek. My tiger was still conflicted about killing a fellow Justice, and his Council's apparent withdrawal of their support from him. His feather still hung from his neck, and I often caught him fingering it, with a sad look on his face, in unguarded moments. He'd been busy with the local wolves, dealing with the fallout, sometimes gone for days at a time.

The loneliness came because I knew that time was growing short. Samir would tire of these games, and then we'd find out if everything I could do, everything I had, was enough to keep the people I loved safe. My helplessness against Wylde's stupid witch coven didn't help my confidence. How was I to fight monsters without being the bad guy? How to fight people who weren't monsters, but were just bigots? I didn't think I could kill someone for just being an asshole, much as I sort of wanted to in the deep dark parts of my soul.

But, sitting at the dining table in the Henhouse, listening to my friends scheme and make plans to help me take out the latest big bad to throw himself at us, my loneliness faded into the background. I had some pretty awesome friends and they weren't running away, weren't cowering, or coming up with excuses. They were tackling every problem like proper gamers, as though our enemies were a puzzle that just needed the right solution.

We had to wait until late morning before Yosemite was ready to leave. Alek wanted to come with us, but I made him stay. He'd barely slept in two days and his ribs were poking out. He needed rest and a ton of food. Yosemite didn't have a driver's license, or any ID at all, so I asked Ezee if he'd come to split the driving with me. No ulterior motive there, I swore, ignoring Alek's disapproving face at my lie.

Ezee had an SUV, which would make the trip more comfortable for all of us. I let him take the first leg to Seattle, and curled up across the back seat, pillowing my head on my arms. As I drifted off, I heard Ezee chuckle at something Yosemite said, and I smiled.

"Haruki," soft voices whisper around me. I can't tell where they are coming from. Bamboo towers over my head as I run,

the thin, sharp leaves slicing my bare arms. My heart pounds and my leg muscles are tired. I've come all the way from the village by the sea. Sweat stings my eyes, but I resist wiping it away.

"Haruki, Haru, Haruki-ki-ki," the voices sing out, movement in the bamboo around me giving them away.

Children, I scoff to myself. I am not like them. They can torment me all they like. I am sure Mother put them up to it, another layer of distraction. I shove my anger down, letting it burn inside me, an ember keeping warm for later. Today I do not need it.

The bamboo ends at the edge of a clear stream and I leap over, falling into a silent roll on the other side, and come to my feet beside the walled garden. I lick my palms to ignite the words carved upon them, the fine cuts stinging, and climb the smooth stone wall like a spider. At the top I pause. Below me is the garden, spread in a spiral of careful paths and shaped trees leading to the inner courtyard.

There, standing on the bridge over an empty stream, is my target. The woman stands with her back to me, her long black hair loose over her blue robe. Too easy.

I leap down from the wall, rolling again, and slip the kunai from my vest. I have only one spellblade. I must choose the right target, or I will fail.

Failure has no appeal, no honor. I am a poor loser, Mother tells me. I would always rather win. Wouldn't everyone?

A songbird sings out in a cage on a pole high above as I run by, startling me. The wind picks up, making fallen petals dance along the path.

Another woman waits in the center of the spiral, sitting calmly in seiza, her hands open on her knees, palms facing the overcast sky as though waiting to collect the rain that will surely fall tonight. Her hair is unbound as well, falling over her shoulders like ink spilled from a broken bottle.

I let the kunai fly, my aim true, and it buries itself in her chest with a dull thud.

The woman vanishes, a block of wood with a smoking piece of rice paper stuck to it all that remains of mother's illusion.

The woman at the bridge turns and bows respectfully as she approaches. I have not failed.

"Haruki," she says. "What have you learned?"

"That illusion is immune to wind," I say, unable to hide my smile. "Her hair did not move."

Mother shakes her head, her hair swaying gently with the motion. "I suppose that must be close enough the lesson, then. You must observe, always, Haruki-kun. Very little in this world is as it appears."

I woke from my half-dream, half-memory to find that it was dark out, with large buildings looming around us. I swept the dream from my head, shoving it away to examine later. Living with the echoes of the people I'd eaten inside my brain could get pretty creepy and I wasn't up for dealing with whatever my subconscious was up to right now.

"I thought you were going to wake me to help drive," I said to Ezee, sitting up. "Looks like we are here." I'd slept for nearly nine straight hours, cramped in the car, and I couldn't decide if I felt better or worse. My mouth tasted thick with sleep and slightly sour.

"You looked so peaceful, we didn't want to wake you," Ezee said.

He seemed relaxed, more so than when we'd gotten in the car. I wondered how much of the intervening time he'd spent talking to Yosemite. The druid looked calm as well, and I had a feeling something had been worked out between them, whatever it was. More birds and fishes, maybe. Maybe not. I didn't want to ruin the comfortable vibe by asking personal questions. I could try grilling Ezee about how his love life was shaking out later, in that magical future where someone wasn't trying to kill us.

"Are we there yet?" I quipped, smiling at Ezee as he flicked his gaze to me in the rearview mirror and made a face. I rolled my shoulders. Two nights of sleeping on cold, rocky ground, and now cramped in a car seat, made my muscles do their best Rice Krispie impression. Snap, crackle, pop. I felt old.

"Nearly," Yosemite said.

"There" turned out to be a huge old warehouse in West Seattle. We pulled into the dark parking lot. Ezee turned off the car and pulled out his phone, plugging in headphones.

"You aren't coming up?" I said as Yosemite got out of the car. Salty, cold air from the Sound washed in over us.

"No, just you two. Apparently this guy doesn't like a crowd." Ezee said it in a casual way but I could see it bothered him a little.

"I'd say call me if there is trouble out here, but I'm phoneless."

"I'll hit the horn, no worries," he said. "Go on."

Yosemite hadn't said much about the mysterious owner of the book, only that he was a man known as the Archivist. It sounded ominous.

The warehouse was at least two stories, with dark windows high above and a heavy steel door. The door buzzed as we approached, and Yosemite pushed through it. He led me directly up a metal stair, running lights along the steps our only illumination. I could make out a hall beyond the stairs, with what might have been more doors. The place was cool without being cold, but the air had a slightly dusty quality to it that reminded me of a museum. Or a mausoleum.

At the top of the steps, an ornate wooden door carved with huge Fu dogs stood partially open. As we stepped through, lamps came on around the room. Shelves lined the space, stretching up into the shadows, with tall library ladders adorning them in regular intervals. The gentle lamplight gleamed on leather spines embossed with gold leaf and engraved titles. The room was empty other than the books, two padded benches, and a small writing desk. Also it was much smaller than the outside dimensions of the warehouse said it should be. Like a reverse Tardis.

I looked around for doors, but saw none. There must have been more rooms on this level, I was sure of it.

Movement caught my eye and I realized a man stood just outside a pool of lamplight, watching us. He'd moved deliberately, I felt, just enough to catch our attention.

"Archivist," Yosemite said, inclining his head in greeting.

The man stepped into the light. He was slender with an angular, not quite pretty face. His eyes were eerie, a flat, inhuman silver, with pupils that looked more catlike than round. He motioned to the benches, watching me intently. I felt like the mouse and it didn't feel good.

Going on instinct and probably no little amount of nerves built up from the last few days of fighting and running for my life, I sent a light brush of magic at him, trying to discern what he was. His flat silver eyes watched me and his mouth curled in the hint of a smile as nothing happened. I might as well have brushed my power against the desk at his side, or the books on the shelves.

Or a corpse. I listened, using my magic to enhance my senses. The Archivist stood still, too still, frozen like a mannequin, no hint of breath or normal movement to him. No heartbeat.

"Curiosity is known to kill cats, Ms. Crow," he said, raising an eyebrow in a gesture that looked utterly practiced and precise.

"Satisfaction brings them back," I said, letting go of my magic. I didn't want to accept what my brain and senses were telling me. "Do you sparkle in sunlight?" I asked.

"No," he said. "I burn."

I looked at Yosemite, who had seated himself on a bench and was watching us with a guarded, bemused expression. "Great. First unicorns, now vampires. What's the next not-so-mythical thing we can encounter this week? Bigfoot? Ooh, I know! How about a dragon?" I looked back at our silent host.

He had a very strange expression on his face and I had no idea what it meant. "Please," he said after a moment. "Sit."

I sat, realizing I was ranting a little, and tried to get control of my nerves. I was dating a perfect predator, for Universe's sake. This guy was scarier. Shifters I knew: I'd grown up with them. A vampire? I had no idea what was myth and what was reality. It was becoming quite clear to me that there was a lot about the world, the magical world especially, I didn't know. I felt very small all of a sudden and it made me want to lash out.

"Do you have a name?" I asked, trying to curb my tone to something polite.

"Noah Grey," he said, and this time his smile reached his eyes, briefly. I wasn't sure if that was scarier.

Yosemite gave a start of surprise next to me when the Archivist answered, but recovered quickly. "We would like to read the book I discussed."

"All information can be had, for a price," the vampire said. "I doubt you can afford this one."

"I do not want to take the book, only to let Jade read it." The druid was prepared for this. He had a small bag of various rare and special plants and seeds. "I am willing to trade, so we may read and copy what we need."

"A week," Noah said, looking at me. "I will take a week of your time, working for me here. Then you may copy the pages you want."

"What?" I said. I leaned back on the bench and folded my arms over my chest, aware it was a defensive position and not caring. "We don't have a week. And what the hell do you want me for?"

"I have books that even I cannot read, information hidden from me. A week of your time to translate certain texts, is that so much?" His smile was back, this time revealing a hint of sharp white teeth.

"Yes," I said. "For one, we're sort of on a clock here. For another thing, how do you even know I can read the things you want me to translate?"

"But of course you can," he said, tipping his head to the side.

I wished he would blink. His unwavering stare was fucking unnerving. I couldn't help but bend forward, searching his face for a clue as to his thoughts. What did he know about me? How did he know about my gift with languages? Yosemite had promised he would only tell the Archivist that I could read the book and I trusted the druid's word.

"How do you know that?" I asked.

Samir's dagger chose that moment to fall right out of its ankle sheath and clatter to the smooth wooden floor.

I didn't see Noah move. One breath the vampire was standing by the writing desk, the next he knelt in front of me, the dagger in his hands. He turned it over and over and then looked up at me. I tried not to flinch.

"Sorry," I said, reaching for the blade. "It does that."

"As well it should," he said, standing up at a more human speed. He kept a hold of the knife. "This blade is not complete without its twin, so it will always seek to leave its bearer unless he or she holds both."

"What is it, besides mine?" I asked, emphasizing the "mine" a little and holding out my hand. I hoped that Samir didn't have the twin. That would be awkward. The dagger was scary enough on its own.

Reluctantly, Noah handed me back the blade. "What will you pay for that knowledge?" he asked.

I almost said "What do you want" but realized the answer would probably be something like "Another week of your time." I thought about pointing out I had paid translation services easily available on the web, but if this supposed knowledge broker couldn't figure out that much, I wasn't about to share. Maybe later, if I felt like ever dealing with him again, which I really kind of didn't.

"Look," I said, standing up. Noah and I were almost of a height. "We aren't going to loan you my time for a week. We can't. And I'm not going to play these stupid bargaining games. Lives are at stake here, which I realize dead guys probably don't give a flying fuck about, but we need to read the druid's book."

"Trade me the dagger," he said.

"Give us the book, outright," I countered. "Not just to read, but for Yosemite to keep. It should be his, after all."

"Done," he said.

I couldn't repress a small jerk of surprise. I hadn't expected him to cave like that.

"Won't the dagger just try to leave you, too?" I asked as he turned and walked to the desk, pulling a receipt book from one of the little drawers.

"No," he said. "I possess the twin." This time his smile was all teeth.

I bit back all my other questions and glanced at Yosemite. He hadn't said a word in minutes. He stood slowly and shook his head at me, but I sensed a part of him was pleased at the bargain. Why should he not be, right? I'd given something up, not he.

I hated that dagger. I carried it on my person, despite its many attempts to get left behind, dropped, or lost, because I wanted to keep it close, keep it out of the wrong hands. I wasn't sure a vampire constituted the right hands, but he wasn't actively trying to kill me, so I was pretty sure that made him a better candidate for holding onto the thing than most of the other people who knew about it.

Noah signed a receipt, listing one druidic tome for one dagger, magic, and handed it over. He disappeared through a sliding bookcase door at the back of the room, leaving us alone.

"That was probably a mistake," I said quietly to Yosemite.

"Perhaps," he said. "The Archivist is not good, but he is not so bad, either. He lives for the preservation of knowledge, all kinds. Objects, rumors, myth, prophecy, art, literature. It all flows through here and he squirrels it away, a lot of it. Often the most dangerous things. That knife will likely never see the light of day."

"Well, sure," I said, trying on a smile. "Daylight burns that guy, don't you know."

I paced the room as we waited, thinking that Ciaran would have been doing a jig in here if these titles were authentic. I feared touching some of the books, not knowing if the bindings were just decorative or if they were as old as they looked. I found one, a slim volume with a red leather binding and an inlaid figure of an oriental dragon. I reached for the book, forgetting my caution, but Noah returned before I could pull it from the shelf.

"Curiosity and cats, Ms. Crow," he said, clucking his tongue as he walked by me, hauling a thick tome in his arms.

The book was a good foot across and nearly as deep. The cover was carved-wood inlaid with semi-precious stones, and I could almost smell the age of the vellum inside. Knotwork illuminated the first few pages as I pulled my sleeve down over my hand to protect the pages from the oils on my skin.

"It's magically protected," Yosemite said, peering over my shoulder. "Your hands won't hurt it."

"How did the other two get destroyed?" I asked, flipping a page. There were many drawings, diagrams with notes on plants, animals, even a star chart. Something about it was familiar. The book reminded me a little of pictures of the Book of Kells I'd seen online, but not quite so ornate.

"Witch hunters," the druid said, pain straining his voice.

"The Inquisition was not a good time for magic," Noah added. He almost seemed to sigh. "Do you wish to read it here?"

"No," I said. I'd paid pretty dearly, probably more than I knew, for this book. I could read in the car on the way back. I couldn't get motion sickness. "We don't have time."

The vampire walked us to the ornate doors.

"Nice to meet you," I said, trying to sound at least halfway sincere.

He took my hand, his fingers strong and cool against my skin, and bent over it before I could react, brushing his lips against my knuckles. "Until we meet again," he murmured so low I thought I imagined the words—until I saw the predatory look in his strange silver eyes.

I won't say I ran down the steps, but hey, we were in a hurry, so taking them two by two was perfectly natural, and not all because the vampire gave me the heebies.

Ezee was relieved to see us and swore that as long as we grabbed some of Seattle's finest coffee, he was good to drive back as well, so I could read the book and find the rituals we needed to stop Clyde and save the trees. I gulped down scalding coffee after we hit a late drive-through, and dragged the huge book onto my lap, summoning light into my talisman to read by.

The text wasn't easy to read. The handwriting was precise but like many things from its time, the script was difficult to decipher and it was written in about four different languages, only three of which I'd ever seen before. If my gift hadn't been wholly magical, I would have been screwed. Fortunately, magic saved my ass as soon as I stopped squinting so hard and trusted my ability to let me read and make sense of what I was reading. Slowly I grew used to the druid's handwriting and odd diction, and the words and phrases began to make more sense. I shoved away the nagging feeling of familiarity and searched each entry, looking for references to Balor, hearts of the forest, and other keywords. I wished the damn thing was digitized so I could have just used a search function and lost about ten minutes musing if I could create a spell that would hunt the text for me.

Unfortunately, I didn't want to risk messing with the magic preserving the book, or risk the book itself if my spell went sideways somehow, which new spells of mine often did if they were detailed. Settling back against the seat, my thighs growing numb under the weight of the tome, I turned page after page. I found the ritual I thought we needed after over four hours of carefully searching the book, and a lot of pieces fell into place.

"Drive faster," I told Ezee. "We better hope the unicorn is still safe."

"No one has called me," Ezee said. "I'm sure they are fine."

So, of course, no sooner were the cursed words out of his mouth than his damn phone began to sing "Lean on Me," which was his ringtone for his brother.

Levi hadn't meant to call Ezee. Exhausted from keeping watch with the wolves, he'd tried to shut off his phone before he crashed for the night, and hit redial instead. Gave us all heart palpitations.

After pulling over and managing to call back and figure all this out, I made Ezee switch seats with me and drove. I explained to Yosemite what I'd read, promising him a full translation of the ritual later. He listened with the patience of an oak tree, asking me minimal questions, seeming to understand what I was saying better than I did. Which was good, because while I could read the words, that didn't always mean I knew what they were talking about without greater context.

It was early morning when we reached the Henhouse. We needed more sleep, and to prepare. Yosemite had certain plants to gather as well. I wished I understood what needed to happen enough to just magic it into being so, but the book was by druids, dealing with druidic magic. I wasn't sure I could eat a druid's heart and gain his power. Probably. Even the thought was unnerving and I shoved it away, climbing into bed next to Alek.

"Briefing at high noon," I murmured to him, curling up against his warm chest.

"Read the book?" he asked.

"Brought it back with us," I said. "I had to trade Samir's dagger to a vampire for it."

"Vampire? They don't exist." He shook his head and ran a hand down my spine, tugging at my braid where it ended at my waist.

"Yeah, turns out they do."

"You are telling the truth," he said.

"Hey, it happens on occasion."

"I like the druid," Alek said. "I am glad you and Brie are no longer fighting."

"Where is Brie?" I hadn't seen her or Ciaran when we got back.

"Patrolling. She is different, somehow. I can't place it. Even her scent has changed. It is like she is different person."

"Yeah," I said. "I guess a lot of us aren't exactly what we first seem." I was thinking about myself, but also about Tess. Even Alek had given me a very different impression when I'd first met him.

I rubbed my nose in his chest hair and breathed in his vanilla and spice scent. This was home. This was safe. We had the book, we had the ritual, and we had the unicorn. Later today we could end this whole mess. I could take out Clyde, which would be some kind of blow to Samir at least. And there was enough time for me to cuddle with a handsome man who loved me. It was a win all around, so far.

I lay there for a while, feeling like something was terribly wrong. Maybe I was just not cut out for winning.

Unable to sleep, I went down to see Tess after Alek got up to get breakfast. She was still propped up in bed, watching *Farscape* on the TV. The sun was out, streaming in through the light blue curtains, bathing the room in gentle golden light. Tess looked thinner but her smile was strong as she paused the DVD and motioned for me to come sit in one of the chairs pulled up by her bed.

"I see my friends got you hooked on science fiction," I said, closing the door behind me.

"I never watched a lot of shows before. Mostly news shows and occasionally that reality TV junk, so I could keep up with fashion, slang, and that stuff." She lifted a thin shoulder in a half-shrug. "Harper promised that this show has more than one season."

"Oh, it does." I sank into a chair, my back to the window so I wouldn't have to squint at her.

"So far it is funny," she said.

"You must be watching the first season." Harper was evil. I had almost been jealous that my friends were bonding with Tess so well, but they were doing their own version of nerd hazing, from what I could see. Trial by fire. Heartbreaking science fictional fire.

She looked at the TV and then back at me. "You didn't come here to talk about television."

"I met Clyde," I said. My brain had been turning the experience over and over, searching it for meaning. The wrongness started there, I was sure of it. I just couldn't find it. Clyde had been exactly as Tess had described. Flashy. Arrogant. Utterly evil. "He knows you are here."

Her gaze sharpened and she pressed her lips together, nostrils flaring. "I guess I'm not surprised. Samir will know by now I'm gone and I told you he has eyes everywhere."

"He told me you would betray me," I said.

"He doesn't understand why I ran," she said with a snort. "All he sees when he looks at Samir is a handsome man who lets him get away with murder."

"How did you know who Samir really is? What he intends for you both?" I knew how I had discovered it, but I knew too how seductive and sweet Samir could be. Tempting with his offer of knowledge, binding you to him with promises, playing to your strengths and flattering your ego until you felt like you were the most special person in the world. It was a hard thing to break away from, to see the rotten core of him, covered in so many layers of deception. Samir was the best manipulator of desire and fear I'd ever met.

"I've always known," Tess said, closing her eyes. Her voice took on a tight edge, as though her throat hurt. "I watched him kill my grandmother when I was a little girl."

I waited, saying nothing, watching her face as she visibly struggled to control her emotions.

"She was so beautiful. Said that God had given her a gift and she was going to use it. She could heal, you know. She hid it with herb lore and such, but she had a magic touch. No one dared call her a witch—she was too sweet, too kind. Too devout. I think she scared the priests, even. They called her Sister Mary, even though she wasn't a nun. Everyone thought she was my mother, but she'd come and taken me away from Papa after Mama died giving birth. She could do more magic, though. I remember how good she was at hiding things, hiding people. She helped slaves escape along the Eastern Shore, sometimes hiding whole boats in Chesapeake Bay."

Tess stopped and took a deep breath. I waited again to see if she'd continue, but she opened her eyes, now bright with unshed tears, and shook her head.

"Why didn't he kill you?" I asked.

"I don't know," Tess said. "I've thought about it over and over. He looked right at me after he ripped her heart out, though Grandmother hid me under the bed. She had a spell on me, I know that, but he bent right down and looked me in the eye. I remember the blood on his lips, and how my chest was too tight, how I couldn't even scream. Then he smiled and got up and left. Just like that." Her hands fisted in the quilt and the tears spilled from her eyes.

I got up and found her a tissue. She was a crazy-strong woman. I'd been with Samir because I hadn't known better. The moment I figured out what he was, what he intended, I'd be so damn pissed I'd confronted him, and when it became clear he was too powerful to face, I'd run. Tess had waited over a century, and when faced with him again, she'd pretended to be naïve, new, just a young sorceress waiting for him to fatten and slaughter. I had to admire her survival skills, her patience.

"You really want him dead, don't you?" I said softly.

"Yes," she said, her brandy-colored irises catching the sunlight, the highlights in them like sparks. "It was almost a relief when I realized he was close to finding me. I was teaching pottery at an art school and had to use magic to save myself when the kiln exploded. I knew it was enough that I was likely exposed."

"Why come to me now?" I asked. I'd asked her before, but I wanted to hear it again.

"You hurt him," she said. "And he is getting moodier, more paranoid. Clyde, too. I felt as though his games with you are coming to a close. So I took my chance." She rubbed her fingers over the crucifix charm on her wrist in a gesture that reminded me of how I touched my talisman for comfort sometimes.

"You are Catholic?" I said. "After all you've seen, you believe in God?"

"You believe because you have seen. Blessed are those who have not seen, and yet believe," she answered, the words sounding old-fashioned.

"Scripture?" I guessed.

"Jesus Christ spoke those words to Thomas the Doubter. I guess your people have their own god, right? A Great Spirit?" She closed her hand over her bracelet, as though wanting to hide the cross from my heathen eyes. I got the feeling I'd annoyed her.

"Sure," I said, mildly annoyed myself. "My people, as you put it, are totally homogenous just like you white folk. We all have the same culture and believe exactly the same things."

"Touché," she said. "I'm sorry."

"No," I said with a sigh. "Don't be. I was raised in a cult, pretty much. Our god, if we had one, was my grandfather. He preached that the perfect spirit of the Crow had to be preserved, that crows and wolves and men didn't share beds or homes, but each kept to their own. He did pretty awful things to cleave to his vision of how things ought to be. All religion seems to bring people is fear, hatred, and just as dead in the end. I have no use for it."

"No faith in anything greater than yourself?" she said softly. "It sounds lonely."

"I guess I have some kind of faith. I believe the universe is vast and that there are many things I don't understand."

We sat quietly for a little while, her rubbing her crucifix, me trying to figure out why I was so prickly, what felt off about everything. Nerves before battle, perhaps.

"How did *you* find out what Samir intended for you?" Tess asked me after some minutes had passed.

I dragged my gaze back to her face. She watched me intently, almost disturbingly so, but I shoved my feelings away. I was getting pretty good at it.

"I read his diary," I said. "He was pretty clear in his thoughts and feelings on the matter. And he'd done it before, kept a catalog of who and when and what he felt he'd gained from the experience." The experience of killing and eating heart after heart.

I didn't admit that I'd not read as closely as I wished. I'd been in shock, sitting alone in the big library, holding the book I'd pulled off the shelf in my hands, disbelieving that what I was reading was real. I'd slammed through all five stages of grief real quick that day, though I wasn't sure I'd ever hit the acceptance phase. Pretty sure I got stuck on anger.

"You could read his journals?" Tess said.

"They were just there, not hidden or anything. He went away for a few days and I got bored, so I snooped. I stayed away from the older ones, since he had spells on those, but the last couple notebooks were right there for the taking." I knew I was avoiding answering the question she had actually asked, but I didn't feel like broadcasting my language abilities. Even with her injured in bed and her apparent friendliness and sincerity, I couldn't quite bring myself to trust her. Not yet.

I wondered if Samir still kept the journals out. If he still had a library. He'd had a wonderful collection of books, some dating back hundreds of years if not further, beautiful books like the one we'd traded the vampire for. I'd spent hours in that library whenever Samir had to go away for business, often sitting with gloves on in the temperature-controlled room and flipping through old volumes of poetry and lore.

Old books. Like the druid's book. I forced myself to stand up slowly, not leap and run for the door even though adrenaline slammed into my veins.

"I'm going to get some breakfast," I said. My even voice sounded normal. Go me. "Want me to send in anything? Or do you feel up to coming out?"

"The bathroom trip nearly wiped me out," she said with a small smile. "I'm okay. I'll just keep watching this show. Let me know what the plan is though. I want to help if I can."

"No problem," I lied. "I'll let you know."

I left the room and ducked down the hall out of sight of everyone. Sagging against the wall, I closed my eyes. I knew why the book was familiar, and with that knowledge other things started to topple into place.

I wanted to be wrong. Because if I was right, we weren't winning at all.

I pulled Alek away from the breakfast table with only minor teasing from my friends. Yosemite was outside, standing just beyond the garden in the trees, apparently talking to a birch tree.

Alek set up a ward around us and I laid out my suspicions, and my plan.

"It's a lot of guesswork," the druid said, running a hand over his thick red beard.

"Jade has good instincts," Alek said, surprising me with his quiet defense of my theories. I hadn't always been right about things and he'd been around to witness some of my worst mistakes. Still, his support warmed me better than the morning sun.

"If I'm wrong, we can still get to you to help in time. If I'm right, it will take the pressure off you and allow you to fix the forest and lay Balor back to rest."

"Why Brie?" he asked.

"I saw what she could do with that sword. Also, I trust her not to do something stupid and get in over her head trying to protect me."

"Unlike, say, Harper," Alek said with a rude snort.

"She's got that foxy courage—what can I say?" I smiled at him.

Harper was my best friend, but no way could I trust her to go with this plan if she knew the truth. The very friendship that bound the twins, Harper, and I together would potentially give the game away and get them killed.

If I was right. I really wanted to be wrong, but the pieces fit into a picture we couldn't afford to ignore.

"Ciaran must stay near Brie, if she is to fight," Yosemite said.

"If they agree, he can come." I had considered bringing Ciaran into this meeting. I trusted the leprechaun to keep a secret. He and Brie weren't back yet, however, and I couldn't let the plan wait. Our noon meeting was coming, and the three of us had to be in agreement.

"And you are sure they will not see through the ruse?"

I was going to rename this guy Thomas the Doubter. Geez.

"No," I said. "The book is written in Old Irish, Middle Irish, some weird-ass dialect of Latin, and a bunch of words in something the weird part of my brain tells me is called 'Stone.' I doubt it is something anyone besides me could totally parse, but there's enough recognizable there that someone with enough knowledge could maybe make out the meanings." I wondered if humans had been misunderstanding the phrase "written in stone" for centuries, but I shoved that thought aside.

"I cannot say, but that I hope you are wrong," Yosemite said. "These games within games are tiring to even consider." He shook his head and rubbed at the bridge of his nose as though he felt a headache coming on.

"Hope for the best," I said. "Plan for the worst." It was all we could do.

"This plan sucks," Harper said.

We had gathered in the living room like a ragtag band of adventurers. Rosie hovered at the edge, teacup in hand. Max and Aurelio sat on the floor, heads tipped in mirrored gestures of consideration. Harper sat with her feet pulled up in one of the overstuffed chairs, glaring at me. The twins were side by side, Ezee watching Yosemite's face with narrowed dark eyes, Levi sucking speculatively on one of his lip rings. Junebug sat next to her husband, her fingers laced with his. Brie leaned against a wall behind Harper's chair and Ciaran hovered near her, his red coat bright as fresh blood in the sunlight streaming through the window next to him. Only Tess was missing, but her door was open and I knew she could hear what we said.

I stood at the end of the room, flanked by Alek and Yosemite.

"It's the plan we have," I said. "We have to divide ourselves if we are going to do both rituals. We can't have the magic interfering, and we can't provide one big juicy target. It's not that bad a plan, come on."

"Whatever. I'm going with you." Harper folded her arms over her knees.

"No," I said, too sharply. I sucked in a breath and forced myself to calm down. "What I'm doing is the more minor thing. Alek, Ciaran, and Brie should be enough. We'll have to be quick and quiet, and we want to distract Clyde with the larger force. That's why the rest of you need to go protect the druid. And Lir. He's the last unicorn, after all."

Cheap shot on my part, but it got Max and Levi both nodding. Harper made a face at me and rolled her eyes.

"Fine," she muttered.

"Great," I said. "Arm up and let's go do this thing. We have to be in place by twilight."

Orders issued, objections quelled, the group broke up into smaller groups. Brie came over to me, her eyes searching my face. When she spoke, however, it was to Yosemite.

"You trust her?" she asked him in Old Irish.

"Yo," I said. "Standing right here, totally understand you."

"I do," Yosemite said, as though I weren't standing right here, totally able to understand them.

"There are many here who think you are worth following, Jade Crow," she said, looking at me now.

It wasn't my imagination, or Alek's. Brie was different. She looked a decade younger and her eyes were full of power, her gaze keen as a sword blade. The gentle, helpful magic she infused into her baking was nothing like the hot, sharp power that rippled off her in lazy waves.

"Who are you?" I said, sticking to Old Irish, aware our conversation could be overheard.

"E pluribus unum," she said with a toothy smile that didn't reach her eyes. *Out of many, one.* Like it explained anything. Ha.

"Okay, then," I muttered.

"Brie," Ciaran said, tugging lightly on her sleeve. "Come."

He led her away. Yosemite followed them, leaving Alek and I almost alone at the edge of the room.

"Tell me I'm doing the right thing," I whispered in Russian.

"You are worth following, kitten," he said, wrapping his arms around me.

Not what I'd asked for, but somehow it was the right thing to say. I squeezed him back and then went to prepare for the worst.

"I'm going with you," Tess said to me as I went to say goodbye to her.

She was up, leaning unsteadily on the bed, and trying to pull a sweater over her head. She'd definitely lost weight. Healing was apparently far tougher on her than on me.

"Fat chance," I said. "I mean this in the nicest way, but you aren't strong yet. Worrying about you might get us killed."

"I'm stronger than I look," she said.

"Says the woman who can't pull on a sweater without looking like she's in agony."

"I want to help." She dropped the sweater and glared at me. "Besides," she added, her expression shifting from anger to worry in a blink, "what if Samir comes for me here while you are all out fighting Clyde?"

I'd thought about that. I'd been doing a lot of thinking all morning about Samir, about what I knew of him and how he'd acted toward me so far since I'd revealed myself months ago.

"I don't think it'll happen," I said. "I think he'll sit back, watch to see what Clyde manages with this Fomoire and Balor's Eye crap. Samir likes a show."

She pressed her lips together and nodded. "He does," she admitted. "Clyde might be arrogant and young, but he's dangerous, too."

"So am I." I grinned at her, trying to project more confidence than I felt. Clyde wasn't the only one who could put on a show.

"Still feels wrong to stay and convalesce while everyone else fights," she muttered. She climbed back onto the bed, not quite successfully hiding a pained grimace.

"Someone will need to protect Rosie, Max, and Junebug," I said. I'd used the same argument on Max, only saying Tess, Rosie, and Junebug that time. Rosie had forbidden Max to go, much to his anger, but I agreed with her. He was only fifteen. It was hard to remember sometimes, it felt like we'd all been through a lifetime of battles these last few months.

"True," Tess said with a sigh.

I sat on the edge as she arranged herself. The others were almost ready to go, but I had things I wanted to discuss. So many things. There wasn't time for them all.

"You'll be more help later," I said. "After. I think if Clyde fails here, Samir might come himself. Were you serious about us fighting together? You said you know about magic, that you could help teach me."

"I was serious," Tess said. Her eyes fixed on mine, an almost fanatical light burning in their depths.

Doubt whispered in my heart, doubt about my plan, about the connections I was sure I'd made, about Samir's nature and the nature of Clyde's plan. I pushed them away. I had contingencies for being wrong, thin and weak though the beta plan was. I was running out of time, but there was one thing I desperately wanted to know, and I hoped Tess had an answer for me.

"Do you know if Samir lied to me about how we can't be killed unless another sorcerer eats our hearts?" I spat out the question in a rush, thinking about all the times I'd almost died. The times I should have died. Like when I had thrown myself on a freaking bomb only weeks before.

"I think it is true," Tess said after a long moment. "He's lived a very long time, and we don't seem to age much. I've never heard of a sorcerer killed any other way, but we don't exactly appear very often and we all seem to die only one way most of the time, killed by one man." She looked away from me, one hand rubbing her crucifix, her jaw tight.

"But what sets us apart from human magic users? Why don't we die? Why do we have power at our fingertips for asking when others must earn it?" I wanted to know what we were. I wanted to know how it all worked, how much of what little Samir had told me was the truth. I'd eaten the hearts of two men, men who had had to train and learn and steal their power from other things. I knew they were different from what I was; I felt their humanity, their mortality. But my knowledge was weak, blind, like knowing the difference between the taste of licorice and the taste of mint. Two different things, but I didn't know why.

At the heart of it, I wanted to know why I was even more different. Why could I see magic? Why did I heal in hours? Why did I know every damn language?

Why had I survived when so many others had not? Why was Wolf with me, and how had she scarred Samir?

I curled my hands into fists, feeling like a small child. All why and no answers.

"I don't know," Tess said. "Why is there magic at all? I give those questions up to God. It is more peaceful to accept His will than to doubt."

"Don't you want to know why we are what we are?"

"No," she said, her voice soft, her eyes bright in the sunlight as she stared out the window, not meeting my gaze. "I only want to live, to be free of Samir. To let this cup pass from me."

I knitted my eyebrows together, trying to place where I'd heard those words before. More scripture, perhaps.

"We'll find a way," I said, sounding more confident than I felt. "First I'm going to go pwn that brat of his."

"Pwn?" Tess said, finally looking at me again. "Like your shop?"

"It's from the Welsh," I joked.

"Wouldn't it be pronounced *poon* then?" Her expression was skeptical.

"Damn, foiled again," I said.

Alek tapped on the door and stuck his head in. "We are ready," he said, eyes flicking between Tess and I.

I stood up. We were out of time.

Be good, I thought, almost speaking the words aloud.

"Be safe," I said instead. "We'll talk more later."

"Godspeed," Tess said. "Take care, Jade."

The ritual had to be performed in a druid's grove, which was apparently specially cultivated and prepared sacred ground. Yosemite had groves spread across the River of No Return Wilderness, but the nearest to us was a four-hour hike from the nearest trailhead.

The woods were eerily silent, though the day was spectacular, a rare sunny fall day full of color and the crisp promise of winter without winter's bite. No birds sang. No deer flicked annoyed tails at us and ran. It was hunting season; the woods and fields should have been thick with rabbit, fox, deer, bear, and many kinds of birds. It was as though the wilderness itself was holding its breath, waiting to see if we could close Balor's Eye and win the day. As we drew near the grove, I kept an eye on the surroundings, picking out a clearing for later.

The supernatural quiet ended abruptly as we crossed into the grove. It was easy to see where the sacred space started and the normal woods ended. The trees here were taller than any around, their leaves still green as though it were early summer, not nearly winter. A burbling creek flowed along one side of the wide circle of green, whispering trees. Algae formed a soft green carpet at the bottom of the stream, giving the water an emerald cast, and Spanish moss slung from the trees as though shrouding this place, curtaining it off from the normal world.

In the trees around us, giant wolves flowed into position. The dying sunlight coming through the leaves cast heavy green shadows over everyone, except the unicorn. Lir, his body almost unmarred now, followed Yosemite into the grassy center of the grove. The unicorn seemed to understand what was needed. I'd explained the ritual to Yosemite and he'd spoken to Lir in the barn before we left. I watched the beautiful creature as he stood, head up, nostrils flared, watching us all with dark eyes that reminded me for a moment of Wolf's, deep black and full of tiny pinpricks of stars, like a night with no moon.

Alek, Brie, Ciaran, and I stopped on the edge of the grove. Alek clasped forearms with Aurelio before the wolf alpha shifted and went to join his pack. Harper, Levi, and Ezee came to me, shifting from their animal forms to human as they approached.

"You aren't going to change your mind, are you?" Harper said, glaring at me.

"Harper," I said, grabbing her into a hug. "Trust me," I whispered, though with everyone around me having super hearing, there was little point. "Please, furball."

"With my life," she said, hugging me back.

Which was why she couldn't come with me. I wanted to tell her the plan, but I knew she'd insist on going where the real action was, insist on helping. I had to keep my friends out of the way if I could. For as long as I could.

"We get hugs?" Levi said, his grin forced.

"Group hug?" I laughed, blinking against the sudden lump in my throat.

I looked at my friends as they finally let me go.

"Good luck," I said. It was totally inadequate, but I felt like I had to say something.

My merry band of four left the grove behind, backtracking to the clearing I'd picked out earlier. I wanted to be close enough that if I was wrong we could get back to them, but far enough away that if I was right, we'd keep the worst of the danger away. Other than the weird lack of wildlife, there was no sign in this part of the forest of Balor's Eye damaging anything. Yet. Hopefully not ever.

Alek walked beside me, retaining his human form for the moment. I slid my hand into his. He'd argued with me this morning about my plan, but I was firm. I couldn't worry about protecting him and doing what I had to do if I didn't have his promise to stay out of fights that weren't his. He was unhappy, I could tell from the way his shoulders hunched and the grip he kept on my fingers, but he would keep his word. Alek was nothing if not honorable, almost to a fault. I loved him for it, needed it from him. He was a reminder that we could and would do what we had to, but that we could still retain some level of goodness, too, a kind of honor in itself.

We stopped at the clearing and I took my supplies out of my backpack, setting up while Brie and Ciaran looked on. They didn't know the whole plan; they still thought I was doing a ritual. Which I was, of a sort.

Unsure if it was safe to talk out here, though it felt like we were alone in this too-quiet wood, I reiterated my instructions.

"Keep anything that shows up off me, but leave the sorcerer to me. If I fall, run to the others."

"I don't much care for that part." Ciaran shook his head, his silver and copper curls bouncing.

"Makes two of us," Alek said with a growl. Yep, he was still mad at me. Awesomesauce.

"I'm fine with it, if anyone is asking," Brie said. She grinned at me, rolling her shoulders before dropping into a hamstring stretch. "Let the sorcerers duel their own."

"I used to like you," Alek told her, transferring his glare.

"So did I," Ciaran said, though he smiled at her which took much of the sting from his words.

"Jade understands," Brie said.

I wasn't sure I did, but I nodded anyway, my mind already going to what was next. It was a shitty place to be, stuck here with doubts and fears. I wanted to be wrong, but I wanted to be right, too, because it would mean keeping more people safe.

I shook it all off. The sun was setting. Twilight neared. I had to act now, to put on a show for my enemy.

"Places," I said, stepping into mine and gripping my talisman as I summoned my magic.

Alek, Ciaran, and Brie melted into the trees. How half-denuded trees could hide a tall woman with flame-colored hair, a leprechaun in a deep red coat, and a giant white tiger, I don't know. They hid, however. Magic. Fun times.

I started the chant, pitching my voice low and soft, channeling two spells at once. The light dimmed as the sun dropped behind the trees. A breeze picked up, rustled leaves, and then seemed to think better of it. My heartbeat was loud in my ears, pounding in time to my chant. The moments stretched out with no sign of trouble and for a brief second, I felt something like real hope. Wolf materialized beside me, her lips drawn back in a silent snarl.

Then Tess stabbed me in the back.

Or what she thought was me. Her knife sank into the chunk of wood I'd laid out in the middle of the circle I'd drawn in the clearing. The illusion I'd woven with my magic and a little help from Haruki's memories flared purple and dissipated, the glyph burning away beneath her blade.

I stepped out from the trees where I'd hidden, my steps heavy. It was one thing to suspect, another to see without a doubt that I had been right all along. Instead of vindicated or satisfied, I just felt tired and a deep sense of loss over what might have been.

"I believe my line is 'Curse your sudden but inevitable betrayal,'" I said, pulling my power into an invisible shield around me.

Tess yanked the knife from the wood and crouched into a fighting stance, her thin face a picture of surprise.

"How did you know?" she asked.

"What, you want me to monologue and give away all my secrets?" I circled to my right, wanting to draw her gaze and attention away from where my companions were hiding. Tess knew they were there—she'd heard the fake plan this morning, just as I'd intended.

"Humor me," she said.

"Humor *me*," I said, my voice sounding bitter to my own ears. "How much of what you said was lies?"

An expression almost like grief flickered over her face and she straightened up, though she kept the knife in front of herself and stayed light on her feet.

"Not much," she said. "I want Samir dead. I will do anything to accomplish that. I'm sorry."

I believed her, damn her. It was what had made it so difficult to convince myself even when all the pieces started to fall into place.

"Clyde gave it away, or at least set the first real doubt," I said. "When he told me you would betray me."

"You believed him?"

"Yes, and no. I didn't, of course, not after you got half dead saving Levi. But what he said was too on point, too perfect. I wasn't supposed to believe him, was I? He was a common enemy, something to put pressure on us with, someone to confirm through denial that you were genuine."

The last rays of the sun lit the trees on fire and behind Tess I saw movement, something grey and long sliding quietly through the forest. To my left I caught a flash of white in the trees, heading toward whatever lurked there. Tess took the moment of my distraction to attack, her magic flaring cold, warning me.

I poured power into my shield and tried to follow her magic, not her body. She was too fast, warping time around herself so that everything seemed to speed up and then slow down in nauseating waves around me. Her knife bounced off my shield and she retreated as I threw an arc of fire at her, trying to keep it invisible now that I knew she couldn't see my magic.

I'd always envisioned my fire as purple, and when I summoned visible power, it was always purple, too. Mostly because I really liked the color purple. Turning off a thing I'd been doing my whole life was difficult and the streak of flame still had a violet hue to it. She dodged and backed away. We circled each other as something crashed in the trees. This time, I didn't look, but she did, a quick glance and a small smile telling me that she'd been expecting help to arrive for her.

So had I.

"Then there was the book," I said. "And the plan with the Fomoire. From what you'd said about Clyde, from how you didn't know about the unicorns, I knew that you hadn't come up with that part of the plan. So it was either Clyde or Samir or both. Samir has another copy of the druid's book, in his library. I remember seeing it years ago. He wouldn't care about this forest, about the Eye, but he would enjoy something that drew me out, hurt people around me, and distracted me."

"Wouldn't that support me being innocent?" she asked.

"Yes, and no. You were too conveniently timed. Plus I guessed that Clyde was going off the plan, doing showy shit like you said he liked to do. And that Samir didn't tell you the whole of things."

"No," she agreed. "It isn't his way."

"The final piece was how thin you've gotten. You've been healing yourself by speeding up time around you, right? But you can't eat enough to make up for that time, to keep the same appearance."

Her eyes widened and her full mouth curved in a rueful smile. "You learn quickly," she said.

Green light flickered in the woods and the trees behind Tess started to shake and crash into each other. I needed to stop her, end this, before Clyde arrived. I knew my friends would buy me some time, but it was dangerous for them to bait the sorcerer and the stone guardians I was laying a bet on that he'd brought with him.

"No," she said, almost to herself. "He can't have you. I need your power."

Talk time was over. Tess disappeared in a blink, but her magic trailed around her, visible as fine pale blue waves, radiating a frosty chill.

Her knife hit my shield from behind and I threw my weight back as my magic turned away the blade. Alek had loaned me a big Bowie knife, since I'd given up Samir's, but judging from how Tess moved, she was accomplished with this hand-to-hand shit in ways I never would be. I couldn't fight her blade to blade.

I leapt to the side, using my magic to carrying me feet further than my legs would have and threw a wave of fire out from my hands as I twisted. She was too quick for me to aim for, her control of the speed of things around her too good for me to land a blow, so I went for the spray-and-pray method. It was draining and I couldn't tell in the growing gloom if I'd hit. From the singed scent of the air but lack of flaming sorceress, I guessed I'd come close, but had no cigar.

A pale blue wave of power zipped in on my right side and I walled it off with fire. She was too close, and I found myself grinning as I poured magic into the flames, extending the wave as far to each side as I could.

She ran through the flame, bursting into view directly in front of me, her momentum too much for me to stop, too quick to dodge. Her hair caught fire but her knife found my stomach.

Pain seared through me and I lost my grip on my power as I screamed and grabbed at her. I tried to go for my knife, but she clung to me, twisting the blade in my belly. Red spots did a tango across my eyes and my world filled with the scent and sight of Tess on fire, her hair smoldering, her eyes filled with darkness.

I couldn't get away from her, so I clung instead, pushing myself further onto her blade. Her power swirled around us and the fire in her hair went out in a puff of acrid smoke.

"I'm sorry," she said, her face so close to mine that I felt her breath hot on my cheek.

My fingers didn't want to work; my brain was trying to shut down the pain and run screaming into the dark. Numb cold spread from the wound and up into my chest, pushing the pain away, granting me a small space in which to think, to breathe. My hand closed on my own knife and I dragged it free of the sheath. So slow. Still she hung on to me until I weakly shoved her back.

She fell away, just a step. Enough. My free hand closed on the blade in my belly, locking it into place as she tried to drag it out, holding her in place as she kept her grip on it.

I jammed my knife up into her sternum, her own scream ringing in my ears as I cut, throwing magic into the blade, going for her heart. I abandoned the knife as she fell backward, following her down to the ground. I knelt over her as she ineffectually tried to pull the buried knife from her chest. Violet claws grew from my fingers and I plunged my hand into her and ripped out her heart.

Time stopped. The sounds of fighting in the trees died. The air froze and I couldn't breathe for a moment as my body adjusted. Tess's heart in my hand was hot, almost burning me, still beating. Her eyes were open, her pupils huge and black, eclipsing her irises. Speckled with stars.

Her hand, red with my blood—or hers, I couldn't tell—reached up and gripped my own, her silver bracelet shining with its own light, the cross on it a tiny star. She pressed her heart toward me.

"Take," she whispered, the words hardly more than a sigh. "Eat. This is my body, which is given for you. Do this in remembrance of me."

I hesitated, then nodded, biting into her heart, putting out the light in her eyes and drawing it into my own. I'd seen most of the game, played it out almost to the end. As Tess died and became a part of me, her cold power sinking into my own inner ocean of magic, I saw the check and mate.

I'd thought she was lying, that somehow she had managed to deceive Alek, fool his Justice ability. I was wrong, dead fucking wrong.

Tess's memories flowed through me and I saw her choices through her eyes. She was willing to do whatever it took to defeat Samir. She was willing to help me, teach me.

To join her power with mine. Join me.

Literally.

Pain flared again, the numbness burning away as time sped back up and the bubble Tess had cast around us died with her. I yanked the knife from my belly before I could think about it too hard and lose my will. Or consciousness.

I poured raw magic into the wound, visualizing it closing, willing my body to heal. The blood stopped gushing but even getting to my feet was agony. I reached for Tess's cold magic and numbed myself, letting her memories guide me instinctually. It would take practice to learn to do what she had done, but I could mimic what I'd seen, what I'd felt.

The wound throbbed but the worst of the pain faded. Tiger-Alek crashed out of the trees and rolled across the clearing, gaining his feet with a snarl. He spared a glance for me as a huge stone catlike beast followed him, rust-colored smoke spilling from cracks along its body. Blood stained tiger-Alek's white coat, a gash open and oozing along one shoulder.

Trees crashed and shook in the forest and green light flickered in the twilight between the trunks. I thought I saw two women, both with long flaming hair, dancing out there, swords in hand, fighting the stone snake. The trees and growing darkness made it difficult to tell.

"Clyde," I screamed at the woods. I stumbled forward, every step threatening to break the icy magic I had cloaking my wound. I wrapped my hand around my talisman and gritted my teeth. This battle was only half won.

He appeared, slender and shining with dark power, springing from the trees. Tentacles of inky light slashed toward me.

"You killed her," he snarled. "She was mine!"

I slashed out with purple fire, burning back the tentacles. Greasy smoke hazed the air, the smell something between a wet campfire and a pile of rotting garbage.

"Come and get her, then," I said through clenched teeth.

His magic was the filth that had tainted the unicorn, the same oily black sludge now turned into slick tentacles that rent the air with acidic smoke. At the corner of my vision, I watched as Alek sprang at the stone beast. The cat was nearly as big as he was and they rolled back into the trees, a flash of rusty light and white fur.

I wanted to go and help him but I forced myself to stay focused on Clyde. I'd told Alek not to interfere with my fight with the sorcerers when they showed up, and he'd made me promise to let him and Brie protect me from the guardians that I was sure Clyde would bring with him.

I'd wondered if Clyde would bring along the Fomoire hounds as well, but gambled that he would send those at the druid, seeking to keep them occupied so no one could interfere with him and Tess. The Tess in my thoughts whispered that Clyde had likely hoped I would bring her down, or at least drain her low, so he could take her heart for himself. He would harvest mine for Samir, she thought, and in her memories I saw the heart container, a small sliver-threaded bag.

A bag tied now to Clyde's belt. The sorcerer wore a long coat, which he stripped off and dropped to the ground as he gathered more power, circling to my right. Tentacles lashed out from his outstretched hands and again I threw a wave of magic fire at them, shoving them back.

The red-spot tango was back in my vision, the euphoria I'd felt for a moment as I took Tess's gift to me now drained completely away. I had no time to prepare for the tentacles; he was able to move them independently, sending them at me from both sides. I expended blast after blast of sheer raw power, trying to hang on to reserves, to see a weakness, and a way to reach him. I was too hurt to charge him; even sidestepping was enough to cause panic in my body, enough to threaten my balance as my legs tried to give out.

He's so arrogant, mind-Tess whispered to me.

He wanted my heart. He thought he could win, and maybe he could, but maybe I could out-power him. If I hadn't already spent this whole damn week draining myself over and over, if I hadn't been stabbed by Tess, I probably could have. As she'd told me, he was young, inexperienced with doing damage to things that fought back.

He advanced slowly on me, now wielding three tentacles that struck at me from the top and sides.

"Fall already," he snarled at me, his eyes black with his power, filth emanating from him in sickening waves. And I saw my opening.

So I took it. I fell, dropping to one knee, turning my power from offensive into a shield along my skin, keeping the filth off myself but letting it batter me, drive me to the ground. I used my body to shield my hand from Clyde's line of sight as I picked up Tess's knife, still wet with my blood. Then I waited.

Maybe I really was some kind of Super Saiyan. Glutton for punishment and pain, but rising stronger every time. I almost laughed at the mental image of me with white hair sticking straight up but held it in. That was the delirium talking.

Triumphant, grinning, Clyde ceased his tentacle attacks and closed on me, his eyes flicking around the clearing to make sure we were alone. A terrible battle raged in the trees but our space was open, only growls and howls and the breaking of branches and shaking of limbs giving any sign that we weren't wholly alone out here.

He stepped in close enough, only a tiger's length away now. I sprang, ignoring the pain in my belly, ignoring the darkness tugging at my vision. I used my magic to shove me forward and flew through the air, slamming into him. We rolled. I stabbed at him, over and over, eyes squeezed shut, mouth closed against the inky putrid magic leaking from him. He panicked and tried to use his hands, his body, losing his grip on his power.

I sank the knife into him again and again, throwing my own magic along the blade, searing into that darkness, remembering how it had nearly killed the unicorn's wondrous light. Clyde stopped struggling and his screams died. My knife had found his heart.

Rolling off him, I lay on the grass. Stars winked down at me. Wolf appeared, her cold nose sliding under my hand as she crouched beside me. My own breathing was labored, heavy.

Clyde's breath gurgled, erratic. He was still alive. I hadn't taken his heart yet.

Green light spilled from the forest as a keening note, high and pure, rang through the forest. The stone cat and a huge turtle insect plunged into the clearing. Their hides were marked with scores and leaking rusty smoke. Three women followed the turtle, tiger-Alek at their side. They could have been triplets, each with long curling red hair and eyes full of emerald fire.

The light followed, first in streamers and then in a tidal wave, swamping us all. The stone beasts fell apart, their carapaces turning to shimmering mist. The three Bries cried out, their voices singing with glory. Behind them, a small, stout man in red ran toward them. Tiger-Alek roared.

The wave poured over and around me. Faces formed and dissipated before I could make them out. I hadn't realized how hurt I was until the pain just quit, its sudden absence making me gasp. Then the light changed from green to iridescent, and the song, that pure, clear note, became wild with joy.

The soul of the wild. I'd touched a piece of it within Lir. It danced and sang around me, awake and free, cleansing the wood of Clyde's filth, closing Balor's Eye.

Tess, built of green smoke and glimmering fire, appeared beside me.

"Take his heart," she said, her voice many voices, all languages, as though she spoke in tongues. My ears rang with the power in that voice.

I crawled to my knees and looked down at Clyde. He watched me with wide, pale eyes as I formed violet claws with magic around my hand. I ripped his heart out with the ease of pulling a half-embedded stone from sand, and held it dripping and beating in my hand.

He shuddered and his eyes bled to black, but there were no stars reflected in them. I started to raise the heart to my already bloody mouth, but stopped.

This would be my fourth heart taken. Each of the others now lived on in me in a way, their experiences now mine, their memories, their abilities, their knowledge. Through me, they survived—even the damned serial killer whose memories I had mostly burned away.

"No," I said. Clyde's power was evil, his knowledge was of evil things, twisted life, ruined spirits. I felt nothing but filth and cruelty from him, in his magic.

I was already killer enough, worried enough that if push came to shove, I'd fall off the cliff of "not quite good" and tumble down into evil in the name of survival.

Mind-Tess railed at me, but the soul of the forest, still glimmering beside me in Tess's likeness, nodded as I met its eyes. I pulled the silver bag from Clyde's belt, ignoring the sweet, familiar feel of Samir's magic. Then I shoved Clyde's heart into the bag, and watched his body still and his eyes cloud over as I zipped the bag shut.

The light took his body, the ground beneath me opening up and sucking him in like shimmering green quicksand. The heart in the bag still beat, but Clyde's magic was cut off, dormant, his body just a body without it.

The wild light faded away, but my own magic burned on, my body light from within by purple fire as I knelt over the bare ground and let my tears fall.

Alek wrapped warm, human arms around me and I opened my eyes. I was no longer glowing and the woods were quite dark. We'd brought flashlights, but they were in a black bag by a tree somewhere.

"The others?" Alek asked.

"The Fomoire are gone," I said, sure of it. "Yosemite finished the ritual."

Alek turned his head even as I spoke, listening to something I couldn't hear. My ears were still ringing from the forest's voice. Ghostly grey and brown wolves appeared and lined the edge of the clearing. They parted and Harper came through, followed by a small herd of unicorns, Lir at their head. The unicorns' coats gleamed like moonlight in the growing gloom.

She limped right up to me as I stood there, my mouth hanging open.

"We won," she said, making it both a statement and a question.

"We won," I confirmed as I tightened my grip on the silver bag.

Harper looked past me. "Who's the kid?"

I turned and saw Ciaran holding a little girl in his arms. She had thick red hair and a confused look on her face. She was tiny, no more than three or four years old. He was whispering quietly to her, the words too low to make out. There was no sign of Brie or her two doppelgangers. He looked up and nodded to us, then disappeared in a puff of gold smoke, taking the odd child with him.

"No idea," I lied. I had a pretty good idea who that girl was, but finding out the truth would have to wait.

"Anyone hurt?" Alek asked.

Ezee and Levi limped out of the trees, both in human form and each favoring a leg. Yosemite followed. He seemed more solid to me, standing even taller. I wondered what the soul of the wild had done or said to him. Whatever it had been, I had a feeling he'd leveled up as a druid.

"We're good," Levi called.

"Is that…?" Harper said, noticing the body crumpled on the ground behind me.

"Tess," I said. "We need to take her back."

My friends looked at me, then at each other. Wisely, they all just shrugged. I knew I'd have to explain Tess's betrayal—or rather, her not-betrayal. Explain how I'd known that Balor's Eye was just a distraction, that Clyde was after me, so I'd baited him and Tess by separating myself from the ritual, guessing correctly that the sorcerers would come after me. They didn't care if the druid won his fight or not. The deaths of the unicorns had been Clyde playing around, taunting the druid, taunting me. It had helped give away the game, in the end.

"Jade," Alek murmured. "She betrayed you."

"She needs to be laid to rest in a graveyard, a Christian one," I said. "She did what she thought was right. I'll explain later." Hopefully later I'd have figured it all out myself. There was a lot to think through now.

Alek frowned at me, but nodded. "I'll carry her," he said.

I'd been mostly healed by the soul of the wild, but it was still a long, slow journey back to the Henhouse. Levi, Ezee, and Harper were all still hurting, but refused Yosemite's offer to ask the unicorns to carry them home. The forest spirit had healed them enough that they wanted to make the journey. Harper also pointed out that Max would never forgive her if she got to ride a unicorn when he'd been forced to stay behind.

We ran into Max on the way back. Rosie had realized Tess was missing, and Max was trying to track her. He crumpled when he saw her dead body in Alek's arms. I didn't have the heart to tell him she'd betrayed us. It wasn't wholly true anyway. We wrapped Tess's body in clean sheets and laid her in the barn.

All I wanted was a hot shower and a million years of sleep. Tomorrow I would figure out how to break into a graveyard and bury a body. I didn't know any priests, so I asked Yosemite if he would help bury her. He said he knew many Christian prayers and would see if he could find something right to say. Levi overheard us and mentioned he knew a priest and would make a call.

"How tired are you?" I asked Alek after we'd taken a chaste shower together. Mostly chaste. There had been a lot of clinging, as neither of us wanted to break the sheer comfort of skin-on-skin contact.

"What do you need?" he asked, pushing my wet hair back behind my ears as he cupped my face.

I pointed to the silver bag. "Take that; hide it somewhere far away from here or my shop. Don't tell me where it is."

"You didn't kill him," he said.

"I don't want his power. I don't want his filth in me. I know that power is power, magic is magic, that it is all a tool to be used, but this is a tool I don't want. It's an atomic bomb, waiting to destroy me."

"Why have me hide it?" He tipped his head to one side, looking down at me, his expression unreadable.

"I think Samir will come for it." Tess thought he would. I felt her in my head, her memories and thought patterns fresh in my mind. "I think the end game is coming."

"You do not seem afraid," Alek said. "Why not use the heart as bait?"

"I'm too fucking tired to be scared," I said. "But I'll be scared tomorrow. And honestly? I don't want the temptation. If things go poorly, I don't want to have that thing in reach. I don't want to make that choice."

He bent and kissed me softly, his lips warm and slightly chapped. "I will do this for you," he said. "Go to bed."

That was the best suggestion anyone had made all week, so I did exactly as ordered.

Tess was buried properly; an owl-shifter priest from a church over on the Nez Perce reservation presided. Levi and Ezee had a lot of friends. We still had to sneak into the graveyard, a pioneer cemetery, and borrow a grave, but at least we had a real priest. The ghost of Tess in my head was grateful, her churn of memories stilling and her voice going silent for a while after the prayers were spoken.

Rain started to fall as my friends turned away from the old grave. It was one of the most ancient here, the stone worn down nearly to nothing, the grave barely tended. Yosemite had re-grown the grass along the seams of sod where we'd had to displace the earth to lay Tess down. Looking down at the grave, I almost couldn't tell that anyone was buried here at all.

It wasn't right. I shook off Alek's hand as he tried to gently lead me away.

"Wait," I said. "There is something I must do."

I walked around the grave to the headstone and knelt, ignoring the freezing water that seeped immediately into my jeans. I didn't know how to do what I wanted, but I believed I could manage it. Belief would have to be enough.

I called on my magic, thinking of Tess, not as I'd last seen her with blood leaking from her mouth, her chest a gaping wound, her eyes full of the universe. I thought of her smiling, beautiful and delicate, surrounded by my friends. Her memories, what I'd seen of them, told me she had walked a lonely road. While I'd spent my life running from Samir, she had spent hers stalking him, learning what she could while trying to hide in plain sight.

I closed my eyes and sent my magic into the stone, pressing, sculpting, listening to its rhythm and coaxing it beneath my hands. When I finally looked, the light in my talisman revealed new words, carved delicately into the stone, and filled with silver light that only I could see.

RIP Tessa Margaret Haller. She is remembered.

I'd looked up her last words online. They were from the Last Supper, part of the ritual of Communion. She had chosen her sacrifice, believing that I was stronger, that I had a better chance to win against Samir.

She had, in essence, placed her faith in me. Wholly. Irrevocably.

I was going to do my best not to fuck that up. No pressure, right?

After days of neglect and a couple of hexes, my shop was cold and dusty-feeling when I opened it back up two days later. My morning was surprisingly busy for a weekday as regulars came by, asking after my grandmother in a way that had me confused—until Harper showed up and explained she'd spread the story that I'd been out of town most of last week caring for a sick granny. A little cliché of an excuse, but it seemed to work.

Brie showed up with cupcakes and coffee in the early afternoon. I had changed out all the light bulbs and gotten my computer to boot up finally, wondering just how full my work email was now, and dreading finding out.

She looked her normal self, her hair in two braids coiled on her head, her apron dusted with flour. Crow's-feet once against graced her face and her body was stouter than it had been when she wielded a sword.

"Ciaran and Iollan send their goodwill and greetings," she said.

Ciaran, his hair more silver than copper now, had dropped by the Henhouse the day before and told me he and the druid were going to go check and make sure Balor's Eye was shut. They promised to be back within a week. I told Ciaran I'd keep an eye on his shop, but him being out of town for periods of time was normal. Everyone would assume he was on a buying trip somewhere.

"So," I said. Lamest opening ever, but how exactly did one go about asking what I wanted to ask? "You look, well, better. Older again." I could add two and two. Or one and three. I wasn't so ignorant of mythology that I hadn't heard of the Morrigan. I mean, she's all over videogame lore, too. Goddess of war. Threefold goddess.

"I am not what you think," Brie said, opening the lid of her coffee cup and blowing on it.

"So you aren't the Morrigan?"

She laughed, the sound rich and multilayered.

"All right," she admitted. "I'm sort of what you think."

"Iollan called you Brigit, though," I said.

"I was three goddesses once, long before, in a time when we walked among men, spoke with them, were revered. But the old ways are lost. We have dwindled. Brigit, Airmid, and Macha, who you call Morrigan, made a pact, we three. We tied ourselves, our memory, our knowledge, to a young druid, one of the last of his kind, and a young fey, one of the few who remained in this world."

She held up her hand, palm toward me, and a glyph glowed on it briefly.

"A triqueta," I said. The knot was common—an embellishment all over manuscripts, a common piece of tattoo work, too. Yosemite had one right over his heart. Remembering that, I leaned back on my stool and smiled. "Three and one."

"My power is nearly gone. Only our bond holds us together. When I have to use power, I lose myself. I am immortal, in a way, and cannot die, but I become less—we become less."

"A child," I said.

"Ciaran and Iollan guard my memories. They restore me, give me back what I spend, bring me back to life with their belief. There is enough knowledge of the truth of what we were in them to sustain us. For now."

"But people worship old gods, too," I said, still wrapping my head around the idea that I was talking to a freaking goddess. After everything I'd seen this week, it wasn't that tough a stretch, weirdly enough.

"They worship what they think we were. Without knowledge, without truth. The time of gods has come and gone." She shook her head and smiled sadly. Then, rising, she capped her coffee and sighed. "I am sorry I judged you so poorly. It is difficult to hang on to my memories, and the ones that stay are often the most painful. They cloud my judgment sometimes."

"Pretty sure that's normal," I said.

"Perhaps. Well, if you need anything, my door is open to you." She turned to leave but I hopped off my stool and came around the counter.

"Actually," I said, "there is something I need from you."

Peggy Olsen held book group, which was code for coven meetings, in the basement of the library on Wednesday nights. Brie had been reluctant to tell me, but I swore up and down on all the honor I still hoped I had that I wouldn't kill anyone.

Of course, Peggy Olsen and the twelve women of her coven hadn't heard me make that promise.

I had to wait a week longer than I wanted because what I needed was on special order and totally out of season, but I slammed my way into book group in spectacular, showy fashion. Purple light danced along my skin and I'd left my hair loose, expending power so that it floated around me as I kicked in the door and stomped right into the center of the coven meeting, a duffle bag in each hand.

"Stand where you are," I cried out, using more magic to enhance my voice.

The witches froze. Some had been getting coffee from a thermos. There was a long wooden table down the center of the room. On it was a dull ceremonial knife carved from wood. Incense and candles were lit around the room. The witches mostly sat at folding chairs around the table. One looked like she had been taking notes. There wasn't a book in sight. Clearly they hadn't expected anyone to interrupt them or question their cover story. I felt the hum of warding magic, weak but present, as I crossed the threshold. Whatever they'd warded against hadn't included pissed-off sorceresses, apparently.

I memorized each face, recognizing a few. We lived in a small town, after all.

"What do you want?" Peggy said in a shaking voice, finally summoning the courage to rise to her feet.

"I want to talk to you about magic," I said. "I've been reading up, you see. And you all have been terrible witches."

Gasps ran around the room, the fear and tension rising.

"I'm tired of you hexing me, sending bugs and rats and whatever into my business. Harassing my friends. Basically, being annoying little bitches. You know I could squash you like bugs, bring this whole building down, or burn you all to ash where you stand."

I stopped and looked around at them again, meeting each gaze. Only Peggy looked me in the eye.

"But I won't. Because I'm not evil. If you think I am, you need your prescriptions amended, because you have no fucking clue what evil really is. You are dabbling idiots, mistaking a match flame's worth of power for the sun. But you have laws, rules you have to follow. Rules you've apparently forgotten."

I put down the bags and unzipped them. No one made a move to stop me, which showed serious smarts on their side. I wouldn't have hurt anyone, but I'd practiced holding someone in place with magic all week long. Levi, Ezee, Max, and Harper were pretty sick of it. Alek had just raised a pale eyebrow when I'd asked if he would let me practice on him. He was the only one I'd failed to pin for any length of time.

Ladybugs started to flood out of the bag. I prodded them gently with magic, waking them up. I had gone with those because I figured that if any made it out of the building, they wouldn't infest anyone's kitchen or hurt the landscaping. Wylde was going to be free of aphids next spring, for sure.

"I am invoking the threefold law," I said as the little red and black bodies took flight, streaming toward the shocked women. "You want to keep being assholes to me? Fine. Everything you do will come back on you threefold. All of you, since I know without a full coven, there is no way you could raise the power Peggy wields. So think about it before you hex."

Everyone was still frozen in place, staring at me and then at the bugs with shock. Peggy looked like her head was about to implode, her skin turning scarlet.

"Oh yeah," I said, as I turned to leave. I clicked my fingers, sending a low wave of electricity around the room. Witches started cursing as cell phones in purses made terrible squealing noises and died. Acrid green smoke leaked out of Peggy's sweatshirt pocket. "Hexen," I added.

I used my magic to dramatically slam the door behind me as the women unfroze and angry, scared voices started pestering Peggy with questions. I grinned. That had felt way too good. Hopefully it would solve my witch problem. I had a feeling it would. Praise Harper and her clever mind.

"Samir will come for me this time," I whispered to Alek as we lay on the blankets piled across my floor that night. "Tess is sure of it."

"Tess is dead," Alek murmured.

"Not in here," I said, tapping my forehead. "I knew him long ago. She knew him lately. He's grown bored, more bored. Without his apprentices to distract him, and with the lure of Clyde's heart, he'll come himself this time."

"Good," Alek said. "We will face him. You are strong, kitten. And you have many allies."

Great. More people to get killed. I shoved the bleak thought away.

"I just hope it is enough."

"We fight with what we have," he murmured. "Not what we wish to have."

"Okay, Obi-Wan." I nipped his chin and settled into his arms.

"I am not quoting Star Wars," he said, glaring down at me in mock annoyance.

"No, but you sound wise for your years."

"Protect you, I will," he said. "Love you, I do."

We fell asleep, laughter still on our lips.

Alek knew it was not a dream, because in his dreams the world still had smells and tastes. The empty street outside Jade's store was quiet, wind blowing but without bringing scent with it, without sound. He couldn't smell the bakery, though its front door was steps away from him.

A figure walked down the empty street toward him, her shape vaguely female, but shifting, always shifting. Ears of various shapes and sizes came and went in her white hair, her face grew whiskers which were then replaced by soft black fur that shifted to an eagle's beak. The Council had come to speak to him. Carlos had told him once of a visit from the Emissary, but Alek had thought such a thing was far beyond any attention he himself merited.

Once, he would have dropped to his knees in awe. Those days felt far away. Instead he stood and watched the Emissary approach. He had expected this, though he could not guess what the Council would want to show him.

Alek turned his eyes away from the shifting figure and looked up at the dark window above Pwned Comics and Games. In reality, he was up there, his tiger-self curled around Jade's little body, watching over her. His impatience surprised him. This vision might be important. Its timing was no coincidence, not after such a long silence from the Council. He had started to wonder if he were still a Justice, but had pushed away those thoughts, fighting off the dark wave of despair such thinking brought with it.

He could not fight himself forever, he knew. Hard questions would have to be asked, and soon.

Perhaps now.

"Aleksei Kirov," the Emissary said. Her voice was neither male nor no female, a blend of tones and pitch. It had the same chill as night winds on the steppe.

Once, he might have shivered. But he was tiger and had been born to the cold. Here, his heart was colder still, wrapped in a blanket of doubt.

"What do you want?" he said, trying to keep his impatience out of his voice.

"The Hearteater comes for the woman," the Emissary said. "You will give her to him."

He took a physical step back, his tiger rising within, his lips peeling back into a snarl. "No," he said, his voice almost inhuman.

"Look around you."

Alek tore his eyes away from the shifting figure. The buildings now burned, smoke rising, untouched by the odd, steady wind. Bodies littered the street, their blood red like paint, unreal without scent to back it up. Harper lay to his right, her face a beaten mess. She stretched a broken, twisted hand out to him, the look in her eyes one of utter and complete betrayal. Her lips formed words he couldn't make out, the wind taking away any sound she might have made, the vision still silent.

"No," Alek said again. "I will not betray my mate."

"Then they will all die. You will die. Is one life worth so much? You vowed to protect and serve our kind. Would you throw that oath away, throw your life away for a non-shifter? She is not of our kind. She and her battles are not ours to fight."

Alek felt a tightness in his chest. He looked down and watched as a gaping wound opened. There was no pain, just thick spurts of cold ruby blood and a hint of gritty white bone beneath the carved-up flesh. Embedded in his chest just above where the wound gaped, beneath a translucent layer of skin, his silver feather gleamed, infused with power.

He had told Jade once, not so long ago, that he strove for balance. He wanted that feather to weigh more than his soul, when the time came.

"When the time comes," he said softly, speaking mostly to himself, "it will balance."

"You must choose," the Emissary said. "Give up the woman to her kind, and you will save many lives. You are at the crossroads, Aleksei Kirov. You must choose."

Alek willed his fingers to be claws. He sliced his own flesh, digging the feather free. It came out clean and light as down, cool like a snowflake in his palm.

He raised his gaze to the Emissary and met her yellow, cat-slit eyes.

"I have chosen," he said.

Then he opened his palm, and let the feather fall.

If you want to be notified when Annie Bellet's next novel or collection is released, please sign up for the mailing list by going to: http://tinyurl.com/anniebellet. Your email address will never be shared and you can unsubscribe at any time. Want to find more Twenty-Sided Sorceress books? Go here http://overactive.wordpress.com/twenty-sided-sorceress/ for links and more information.

Word-of-mouth and reviews are vital for any author to succeed. If you enjoyed the book, please tell your friends and consider leaving a review wherever you purchased it.